Reviews

I found this book easy to follow. I had no problems with putting myself in there with Jodie and the other characters. This horror story caught me off guard, I developed empathy for Jodie. I found the story was relatable, pragmatic and very understandable. I became sensitive and supportive of Jodie not her actions but felt like they were justified. I would recommend this book to all those readers who appreciate a good horror story.

Lynette.

I thoroughly enjoyed this book. I was engaged from the very first page. I totally identified with the characters and their backstory made it easy to follow along with events. I would recommend this book as I enjoyed reading every minute of it.

Reb.

I don't usually read but this book was easy to follow and kept me on my toes. I loved how this book dropped you straight into the story. It kept me curious of what was to come next. I really connected to Jodie, who is driven by her emotions. I would recommend this book for anyone who doesn't normally read, as it is an easy read. It keeps you engaged and wondering what's going to happen next.

Gemma

Jodie

LUISE COWEN

Jodie
First published in Australia by Luise Cowen 2022

Copyright © Luise Cowen 2022
All Rights Reserved

 A catalogue record for this
book is available from the
National Library of Australia

ISBN: 978-0-646-86795-3 (pbk)

Artwork by L. Vail © 2022

Typesetting and design by Publicious Book Publishing
Published in collaboration with Publicious Book Publishing
www.publicious.com.au

Chapter 1

Jodie was shoved into the small, crowded cell. She took two steps and then stopped, just far enough in for the door to clang shut behind her. She heard the rattle of keys as the door was locked, she looked over her shoulder to see the two Police officers, one male and the other female, turn and walk back up the narrow hallway to the stairs.

Jodie backed up and leaned against the bars. She hadn't been there before. She heard whistles and rude comments from the guys in the opposite cell, across the hallway behind her, and then blocked them out.

The Juvenile Detention Room was upstairs on the ground floor of the Police Station. They weren't segregated like down here in the basement where the adult cells were. On the ground floor there were four plexiglass boxes, also known as "The Fish Tanks". They were where the violent, drunk or substance affected offenders were detained.

1

She had been in one once and actually preferred it to the Juvenile Detention Room. That room felt like a waiting room, with wall-to-wall chairs, benches with clinical white walls and gray linoleum flooring. At least in a fish tank you had your own space and cot. On her way in tonight she noticed that three of them were still empty and she would have preferred to be in one of those than shoved into an adult holding cell. She had taken note of the security cameras down here as she was walked down the hallway. They were probably only there to make sure no one fooled around, used the cells as a toilet or died.

She took it all in from where she stood, not just the women already there but the layout of the cell too. It was maybe ten foot long by seven foot wide. There were only two metal benches, one at each end of the cell – they were full. Those who couldn't get a place on a bench made do with sitting or lying on the dirty cold concrete floor. She was not going to be one of those losers, she waited for an invite. Soon enough there was one, it was in prime position at the end of a bench.

The invitation was made by an older woman who winked at Jodie, licked her lips and then patted her lap. *I shouldn't be in here – let's make the most of it,* Jodie thought with a small smile as she pushed herself off the cold gray metal bars of the cell and walked towards the woman. She had made the same mistake everyone did; Jodie was small but not defenseless.

As Jodie got closer, she noticed the woman had fine brown hair which had streaks of white through it. Her face was tanned a deep brown and heavily lined, being this close Jodie saw how large the woman actually was. Jodie knew she would have to move quickly. She looked Jodie up and down. Jodie remained just out of her reach waiting for the final invitation. When she gave it, Jodie walked towards her, keeping an eye on the woman out of the corner of her eye, she turned as if to sit on the woman's lap – that was when she struck and drove her elbow back and into the woman's face, flattening her nose. Blood spurted out causing those around them to draw back. The sudden sound was deafening as it echoed around the concrete encased basement. Many were screaming and yelling egging on the fight, others were shouting for help to stop it. Jodie took advantage of the extra space and pounced on the woman. She had been distracted clutching her smashed bleeding nose and wasn't ready to defend herself. Jodie grabbed her around the neck and held on. The woman clawed at her arm, kicked and squirmed but Jodie held her in the headlock. Jodie could see the woman's scalp through her hair. She watched as it first turned pink then purple. When she went limp Jodie let go and pushed her off the bench onto the floor. It was almost eerie how all the noise echoing around the basement suddenly stopped when the woman hit the floor.

Jodie took her position in the back corner of the cell and leaned up against the brick wall. She pulled her legs up, putting her feet on the bench resting her elbows on her knees. There was more than enough room, no one was game to get too close. *Just the way I like it* Jodie thought with a satisfied grin. She looked directly into one of the security cameras, smiled and waved. She had hoped that she would be pulled out of the cell and given a fish tank for the rest of the night. The woman she ousted from the bench regained consciousness and sat up. Jodie watched her intently as the woman looked around. She shrugged her shoulders and laid back down, rolled over onto her side and started to softly snore. Jodie turned her attention to the cell door and the hallway beyond. When no officers suddenly appeared, she made herself comfortable. *I shouldn't be here anyway; I was only protecting myself. It's always the same. They smile and be all friendly, like they're earning their good guy chips for Heaven by taking on the Hell Spawn of the Devil and it's never their fault when it all turns to shit.*

Jodie gave herself a mental shake, she couldn't afford to indulge in disappearing into her head. She had to remain vigilant or she might end up on the floor before the night was over. The only sound that echoed around the basement was that of people sleeping. There were sporadic outbursts of loud noises when someone started to snore loudly. They were kicked awake and told to 'Shut the fuck up!'. She wished for the yellowed overhead lights to be switched off but knew for "safety reasons" they stayed on. *Probably a good thing – who knew what might happen in the dark,* Jodie thought to herself with a smirk.

****

She didn't really sleep; she couldn't afford to let her guard down. She had managed to lightly doze but every small noise woke her. She wondered how long she and everyone else were going to be left there. She had been the last in, no more came in overnight. People started to get restless and loudly demanded to use a toilet. A few cheered when they saw two officers come down the hallway. They were the same two from last night that had put her in here, she hoped that they were there for her. They stopped in front of her cell, the guys across the hallway shouted their disgust that none of them were getting out.

'Jodie Marie Sargent' The policewoman said in a slightly nasally voice.

Jodie got up and walked across to the cell door, making sure not to stand on anyone on the floor.

'Turn and present your wrists'

Jodie did as she was told, she backed up to the bars. *They hadn't bothered cuffing me when they brought me down here last night, obviously they have seen my little scuffle. Well, it's good to know that the security cameras aren't dummies and do actually work* she thought as she was cuffed. They weren't taking any chances, once her restraints were secured the cell door was unlocked and opened. It was the male officer who removed her and held her by the arm. His female counterpart closed and locked the cell door. She clipped the keys back on her belt before taking hold of Jodie's other arm as they walked her up the hallway. At the foot of the stairs Jodie looked back and saw no one had taken her spot on the bench. It made her smile. They continued up the stairs to the ground floor and to the front desk, where they stopped and took off her cuffs.

'Go wait on the front steps for a Foster Care Advocate, all the charges have been dropped' the male officer said to her as his partner put her cuffs away. He turned and collected a small clear plastic bag from the front desk officer. It contained her few possessions and he gave it to her before he pointed towards the front doors. She was glued to the spot. *Did I just hear that right, I can just leave and walk out the door, what was the catch?* When she didn't move, he shoved her towards the front doors. She slowly wandered away from him. She pushed open one of the doors, she fully expected to be crash tackled for trying to escape.

Jodie stood on the front steps of the Settlers Cove Police Station, blinking rapidly trying to adjust her eyes to the bright sunshine which made her eyes water. It was already starting to warm up and the sun had only just cleared the deep blue horizon of the ocean. There wasn't a single cloud in the sky but there was a cooling breeze coming off the ocean, it smelt faintly of salt and seaweed. *So good to have that breeze today it'll help keep it from getting hot 'n' sticky like yesterday,* Jodie thought as she held up the plastic bag to make sure everything was there. Once she was satisfied, she stuffed it into her jeans pocket and wondered *would anyone care if I just left?* She walked down a couple of steps and then stopped. She would need a lift back to Martha and Jon Samson's Group Home, all her stuff was there. *How much longer before a bloody Advocate gets here? They'll probably move me again, but where?* While she tried to work out where she could be moved to Jodie wandered down to the bottom step and sat down.

She looked up when a battered brown sedan slowed and then stopped in front of her. The passenger door opened, Jodie got up and went over to the car, peered in and then got in. She could recognize a Foster Care Advocate anywhere. They all had that same look of being both exhausted and frustrated all the time. She put on her seatbelt and then sat silently and waited.

'Jodie, you're probably trying to figure out what's happening...' Marlene stopped for Jodie to reply but she didn't really expect one so she continued 'the charges against you were dropped as you turn 21 in the next few days and will be too old to be in Foster Care. I'm taking you back to Martha and Jon Samson's Group Home to collect your belongings and then take you to Settlers Cove City Shelter' again she stopped and waited for Jodie to reply, Marlene sat there and stared at the small dark-haired girl who looked out the front window silently. Jodie slowly turned her face towards Marlene and nodded once then looked back out the front window again.

Marlene knew that was all she was going to get. 'Okay, Jodie I've already rung ahead to let Martha and Jon know I'm bringing you by to collect your things.' She looked once more at Jodie then put the car in drive and pulled out into the light flow of early morning traffic.

Jodie disappeared back into her head. The only noise in the car was that of the engine and air whistling in through the open windows. *Advocates were all the same, with their sickly pale skin, messy hair and clothes that looked like they've slept in them, but for the bags under their eyes sayin' different. So here we go again, I've suddenly become too difficult. I only fuckin' protected myself! Those pullin' the strings never really want to know the real story. They pretend like they do but really, they don't. Now they're washin' their hands of me by kickin' me out of the fuckin' system. I'm meant to be thankful that I can collect my shit, before I'm dumped with the rest of the homeless and hopeless.* She looked down at her clothes. *I wonder how much of my shit will still be there? No doubt it would've been picked through by now, nobody would be expecting to see me again especially after being taken away in that cop car last night.* Her hand had strayed to the dried blood on her dark blue jeans and she absentmindedly picked at it. The Police had taken her hoodie as evidence. They had given her this horrible brown plaid shirt and light gray jacket to wear. They were huge on her and smelled faintly of cigarettes. There was a smear of dried blood on the elbow of the jacket from last night.

The car stopped and brought her back to the reality of her situation. They were outside the group home. Jodie got out and followed Marlene inside.

Martha and Jon had taken everyone out the back, so no one would see her. That way they could control the narrative and she became the example of what happened when you do not follow the rules. You disappeared. Marlene turned left but stopped at the start of the long hallway that the half a dozen girl's rooms were accessed from; the boy's dormitory was on the other side of the building. She didn't know which room had been Jodie's. Jodie stepped around her and took the lead to her room which she shared with three other girls. Marlene followed Jodie, but once at Jodie's room she waited in the hall. Jodie saw her shit was strewn all over the floor, which helped her with filling her rucksack. She threw in what hadn't been destroyed or nicked. Jodie grabbed any clothing she saw laying around that might fit her and threw that in as well. Jodie looked over quickly at Marlene, she had turned her back. This gave Jodie the privacy to pinch a few things. She took Hattie's stashed cash, along with Lilian's bag of pills and the new girl Peg's snack box. After she had finished filling her bag, she looped the strap over her shoulder and walked back to Marlene. They both walked back down the hallway and out to the car, Jodie threw her bag on the backseat and climbed in the front.

Jodie was driven in silence to the homeless shelter. Once there Jodie got out, collected her bag from the back and expected to see Marlene get out but was left standing on the side of the road. Marlene knew the procedure was to deliver those who age out of the system to admin at the front desk, and fill out the handover paperwork. This started the process of them accessing help to find accommodation and their benefits. It was out of her hands now, she had been told to collect and dump, which she had done. She couldn't really believe what they said Jodie had done. Yet she had seen the blood on the girls' jeans for herself. There must have been so much more to it than she had been told. She knew it would have been useless to ask Jodie, she had grown up in the system and had learnt to keep her mouth shut. Still, to put such a big guy in hospital, she must have been fighting for her life. Marlene looked in her rearview mirror at Jodie.

Jodie stood where she had been left and watched the battered old brown sedan drive away. She turned and looked up at the homeless shelter. It was an old Maine Ranch style home that were still very popular around here. This one though had been added onto over the years, with very little upkeep. Some of the shingles that covered the upper exterior walls had fallen off leaving holes. She looked at the people who were either sitting or lying down on the steps that led up to the front door. She knew as well as anyone who lived on the fringes of society that if the shelter was close to capacity they got picky about who they let in. The overflow camped out on the steps. Those still awake looked like they were either drunk or off their faces on drugs. If the steps were this full already, then after tomorrow night, the fourth of July, there wouldn't be any room to climb them at all, as people recovered from celebrating. Jodie looked at the street sign Hill Climb Way. She realized she wasn't that far from Granny Jo's old home. She turned away from the shelter steps and headed for Granny Jo's.

Marlene took one last look in her rearview mirror and Jodie was gone, she hoped it was because Jodie had gone into the shelter seeking assistance. Her gut said no. She still couldn't get over the fact that Jodie was almost 21, she looked all of maybe 15. Marlene knew that she wouldn't soon forget Jodie's eyes, they were the most piercing blue she had ever seen. The type of eyes that looked through you and into your soul. It had been unnerving to have those eyes look at her. She hoped, like she always did, that this young person's future would be better than their past.

Chapter 2

The day was starting to get warm, yet it was still a nice day for walking. Jodie stopped halfway up the first hill, it was the steepest and highest. She could feel the sweat start to drip down her back. She took off the jacket, put it in her bag and rolled up the sleeves of the shirt. When she got to the top of the hill, the view of Wickleberry brought memories flooding back.

As she continued to walk, her mind wandered back to the beginning. Granny Jo and Grandpa Don married just out of their teens. Grandpa Don was an only child; his parents had passed long before Jodie was born. Whereas Granny Jo's father Norman remarried only a handful of years after his first wife, Athena passed away. Alice, his second wife, had been Athena's nurse and only half his age. It came as a shock to him when he found out that he was going to be a father again. He was over 50. It hadn't been a shock for Granny Jo, she had prepared herself for this outcome from the day her father remarried. She didn't get to see her father much after Wendy, her half-sister, was born. Instead, Granny Jo and Grandpa Don concentrated on living their own life together. They tried to have kids but when it became apparent that they couldn't, they chose to adopt an orphaned two-year-old boy. They named him Lance, Jodie's dad.

Norman and Alice died in a car crash when they were on their way over the hills to visit. Norman had wanted to meet his grandson, Lance. Wendy was only in her early 20's at the time of the reading of the Will. Granny Jo inherited the old house she had grown up in and the Fielder family jewelry. Everything else went to Wendy. After Norman and Alice died, Wendy didn't visit much; she said driving past the site of the car crash made her feel sad and lonely. Which was absolute bullshit as there is more than one road over the hills. Jodie could count on one hand how many times Wendy came over the hills to visit her half-sister, including the visits that happened before she was even born!

Jodie's mom, Gina, had grown up in Foster Care, without knowing her dad and didn't know much about her mom either. Gina had been working as a cleaner at the primary school where Lance was a teacher's assistant. Jodie remembered being told, when her mom and dad planned to get married, that her dad had tried to get Gina to find her mom for their special day, which resulted in a huge fight. Lance had only known and experienced the love within his own small family, but eventually he understood Gina's point of view when she said to him 'The state removed me from her care for my own safety when I was only three and she never tried to get me back. Why would I want that kind of person there?' Jodie started down the other side of the hill. She enjoyed the shade from the old, gnarled trees. They weren't like the perfectly straight and evenly spaced trees that lined Settlers Avenue. These trees had character and helped to keep her cool, which was a bonus as the breeze from the ocean was now blocked.

It wasn't even a year later, when Jodie had been born, their family was complete. Wendy had made the drive over the hills and dropped off several boxes of toys. They had been either hers or Granny Jos, nothing new. She didn't bother to drive back over the hills less than two months later when Grandpa Don had been killed while working demolition. An unsecured wall had fallen and crushed him and two other workers. He was the only one to die that day. There was a pitiful amount of insurance written into his work contract in case he was injured or killed while working.

They weren't in any kind of financial position to afford a lawyer to sue for negligence. Granny Jo had reached out to Wendy for financial help but she had refused. Thankfully, there had been enough public outrage over the incident to get the attention of the big boss. To smooth everything over he had covered the cost of the funeral and double burial plot. He also made sure that there weren't any hold ups to paying the insurance in full.

With the love and support of her new family, Gina graduated from Community College with honors and planned to continue her studies to become a nurse. It was her plan to pay back their love and support by being there to take care of them later. While she was studying, she helped out others where she could. She would baby sit for people like herself, who tried to get an education. It was a cash in hand job, every little bit helped. Nothing they had was fancy but they never wanted that either, they had each other and that was all that mattered.

Jodie looked up and saw she was only a couple blocks away from the house now. Then she remembered the rest of it. The closer she got to the once happy home; the worst memories came back to her.

Granny Jo hadn't been able to bring herself to tell her the truth about what had happened to her parents, she just said it had been an accident. Jodie had heard the full story from Wendy, when she went to live with her. The woman Gina had been babysitting for was in the middle of a violent separation from her partner. He had shown up to get his kid from his Ex, but found Gina there instead. Gina had locked herself in the bathroom and called the Police. She refused to hand over the kid and the guy started to smash his way into the bathroom. He was interrupted by Lance, who fought with him but was stabbed to death. By the time the Police arrived the guy had broken down the bathroom door, shot Gina, his kid and himself. Neighbors had been calling the Police the whole time the incident was happening and still they didn't get there in time. Wendy had finished her version of the story with "if she had just handed over that damn kid, they probably would've survived, and I wouldn't have been saddled with you. That stupid bitch."

There was some sort of inquest because the Police had been called at least an hour before the shootings. Granny Jo and Jodie had been paid some money from the state for their loss. They didn't have much money coming in other than Granny Jo's benefits so that little bit of money was soon spent. Granny Jo would just call it 'the accident'. After she had Lance and Gina cremated, she put their ashes together in a pewter urn which sat on the mantle.

****

Jodie stood on the corner of Humphrey and Walter Streets, looking at the old house. It looked how she felt right then, alone and forgotten about. It was starting to rot, the verandah sagged and some of the support posts bowed, but somehow it still stood. It should have gone to her, but she was only ten when Granny Jo had died suddenly from a heart attack. Jodie walked across Walter Street and up the sidewalk. She looked around but couldn't see anyone on the street or in their front yards, it was now late afternoon and starting to get dark. She pushed on the side gate and surprisingly it opened. She quickly walked through and closed it behind her. She carefully made her way along the cracked concrete path which led to the back door between overgrown garden beds. The path had a buildup of old leaves and twigs but it was mostly clear. At the small porch there was a Honeysuckle which had grown out of an extensive crack in the concrete floor, it had grown up one of the posts and now covered the roof of the porch. Jodie was short enough to not need to duck under the hanging tendrils that were covered in flowers, she reached for and tried the doorknob. It was locked. She bent down and pulled the loose brick out of the wall next to the vent. She felt around inside and found the spare key. It was still there.

She put the brick back and the key in the lock then held her breath as she turned the key. It worked and she breathed a sigh of relief as she shoved the backdoor open. It opened with a loud screech; Jodie froze. She was ready to run if she heard anyone coming. It remained still and quiet. Jodie walked in and stood looking around the small mudroom. The linoleum was cracked, and she could see the floorboards through the holes. She should really close the door. She slowly and gently eased the door closed and it only gave a whimper of a screech as it closed. She locked it.

Jodie leaned against the door letting her bag slip off her shoulder. When Granny Jo died, Wendy had become her guardian and took possession of this house. Wendy didn't like children and never bothered to have any of her own. She loved Jodie about as much as she loved this old rundown house and the shitty neighborhood it sat in. Wendy sold it for redevelopment as soon as she could. It was meant to have been knocked down, but for whatever reason it never happened. The money from the sale was meant to go into a trust fund for Jodie but that never happened either.

Wendy had told the Schoolboard that because Jodie had such a traumatic childhood, she was unable to attend school and that she would be homeschooling her Grandniece. Instead, she became Wendy's live-in slave. No one ever came to see if Jodie was actually being homeschooled. Jodie believed that the large donation Wendy had made guaranteed full agreement from the Schoolboard. They probably thought why would a person with such deep family roots here lie?

At the age of 13 Jodie became a ward of the state. Wendy had gotten rid of her, saying she was unmanageable and unruly. Being in state care had its own challenges but, in some ways, it was easier than the three years of living hell with Wendy. Those years taught Jodie how resilient she could be and the next nearly eight years taught her how to survive as she bounced from one foster or group home to the next. At the last group home, run by Martha and Jon Samson she had proved that she wouldn't let strangers grope her for money. She didn't care that there was never any intercourse, but she was expected to do other things. She had stood her ground and defended herself the best that she could with such a small knife and now she was kicked out of that system.

Jodie looked around the mudroom, it had been cleaned out, anything of value was long gone.

She walked away from her bag and into the kitchen and out of curiosity she turned on the tap. Surprisingly water came out, it was brown. *Good it's still connected to town water.* This made Jodie wonder and she switched on the light in the pantry, and it came on. *Oh, wow that's still connected too.* She noticed that there was still some canned food on the shelves. She would look at that later to see if any of it was still good.

She wandered into the empty dining area, which they had used as their lounge room, even the carpet was gone, it was just floorboards. In the dim light, she could just make out a patch of light-colored ash or soot on the dark slate hearth extension in front of the fireplace and wondered if someone had been squatting here. Then she recognized the top of the urn that held her parent's ashes in the fireplace. Someone had poured out her parent's ashes thinking that the urn held something valuable and when it didn't, they threw the lid into the fireplace and left the ashes where they had poured them out. Seeing this made her angry but also confirmed what she had heard, that Wendy hadn't put anything in storage instead held an open home cash in hand sale. She searched around for the urn and found it in a corner, bent and twisted like it had been stomped on, it was unfixable. She went back into the pantry and found an old mason jar with a lid. It still had some sugar in the bottom. She took the lid off and emptied out the sugar. She tried to make sure it was as clean as possible, with the end of her shirt. She used a flat piece of the urn to scoop up as much of her parent's ashes as she could into the jar. She made sure to put the plaque with their names in there too. She screwed the lid on tightly and walked back to her bag and slipped it inside. She picked up her bag and slung the strap over her shoulder.

Jodie walked from their lounge room into the entryway, the bare floorboards squeaked underfoot. She could have walked the other way through the small hallway, past the room they had jokingly called the study and past the downstairs toilet. She stood at the bottom of the stairs, leaned to her left and looked through the archway into the formal lounge room. The bay window was boarded up, the bench seat under it had collapsed from water damage or wood rot. Jodie turned her attention back to the stairs. She looked up them and wondered if they were safe to use. Jodie gently tested each step before putting all her weight on it, she held tightly onto the railing and slowly made her way up to the landing at the top and was met with four closed doors. To her left was Granny Jo's room, directly in front were two doors, one being her parent's room the other the bathroom and to her right was her old room. She didn't feel the need to go into any of the other rooms, only her own.

She reached out and turned the handle, the door opened easily. It swung freely and quietly open until it thudded against the wall behind it. She could see by the light of the streetlight out front that shone directly into her old room. She only realized then how late it had gotten. She saw that everything was gone, the wardrobe, dressing table, bed frame and toy box. The only things left were her old mattress and the curtains on the windows, which she closed. She shook the mattress to make sure there weren't any mice or rats nesting in it. It smelt a bit musty, but nothing ran out of it. She let her bag slip from her shoulder to the floor and laid down on the mattress. She was home.

Chapter 3

She was exhausted and soon drifted off to sleep. Sometime in the night her stomach rumbled, then painfully twisted which reminded her that she hadn't eaten since the day before. She sat up trying to catch her breath and breathe through the pain. She pulled her bag to her and rummaged around inside until her hand landed on Peg's snack box. It contained an assortment of candies, chocolates and little packets of salami and crackers. It was these that she took out and ate. After her small meal the pain in her stomach stopped, she laid back down and fell into a deep sleep.

Ψ

Jodie had the weirdest dream just before she woke up. She dreamt that in the early morning light her shadow had sat up without her and watched her sleep.

Ψ

She sat up now and looked around her old room in the morning sunlight that peeped through the center gap between the curtains. Everything was gone and yet it still felt like it was her home. She got up and stretched then walked out onto the landing and wondered if she should try and use the bathroom. She opened the door, it looked like it was all there, none of the plumbed fixtures had been ripped out. She hoped that extended to the pipes as well. She opened the top of the toilet and saw that there was water in the tank. She switched her focus to the seat lid and lifted it expecting to find something gross, but the bowl was empty, apart from a bit of discolored water in the bottom. Jodie took that as a good sign and used it, she had been busting. If both of the toilets had been unusable, she would have just pissed in the overgrown garden out back. She pressed the button and it flushed. She stood there and listened to the tank refill; it made her smile. She turned and opened the mirrored cabinet over the vanity, it held a couple of old toothbrushes and a new packet of soap. Jodie noticed all of Granny Jo's medications were gone, but that was to be expected.

She stepped back out onto the landing and stopped outside her parent's room, with her hand hovering over the doorknob. She didn't know why she hesitated; it would only be another empty room. Jodie took a deep breath, turned the handle, and gently pushed the door, hoping it wouldn't open. It swung open easily and stopped against the wall with a soft thud. There was only a mattress on the floor and curtains over the window like her own room. Everything else was gone. She stood there looking at the empty room. After a while she reached in and closed the door again. She turned to Granny Jo's door and before she could second guess herself, she opened that door too.

Jodie remembered that when she had lived here Granny Jo's room was a fantastical place to her with big gold framed paintings of exotic faraway places hung on the walls. There was a huge old four post bed carved from some sort of dark wood with a matching dressing table and huge wardrobe. The wardrobe had four doors, two of them with mirrors on the front and carvings of fawns frolicking with other mythical creatures around the mirrors. The other two doors were carved with geometrical patterns. The bed had what Granny Jo called nymphs playing in a long-lost forest carved into it. Jodie remembered trying to find all the hidden faces in the branches, spectacular flowers and strange fruit. The dressing table had other mythical creatures, but those of the sea, carved into it. Granny Jo's family tree went right back to seafaring merchant times and all these gorgeous pieces of furniture had come down through the family and were hundreds of years old. Wendy never liked them; she said she had found them grotesque. She wondered how anyone could sleep with all those faces watching you while you tried to sleep.

Jodie stood at the threshold looking into the depressingly empty room. She leaned against the door frame as she remembered the history Granny Jo had told her of the area. This area was discovered by a group of half a dozen families looking for their own piece of the new country. Her ancestors the Fielders provided passage to that group and found the harbor here to be deep and safe from the frequent storms that lashed the coastline. They decided to stay and based their trading business from the harbor, which was named Settlers Cove. It became a vibrant and lucrative trading port. About half a century later Settlers Cove was recognized as an established settlement. Ships would dock to trade or seek safety from the devastating storms. There were many rocky outcrops that took ships and their crew along this coastline.

The Fielders decided early on to build their family home away from the port and partway up a hill to capture both the views and the fresh air. The flat land around the port became heavily developed and would often stink from rotting cargo. This part of the coast was late to the age of the locomotive. It had a devastating impact on the shipping trade. Rail Magnate Harold Wickleberry pushed a rail line through the forest and named the station at the end of the line after himself. This side of the hills became known as Wickleberry which experienced its own boom. A side effect of the rail line was more people visiting the coast for the reputed health benefits of being at the seaside. The street out the front of the Fielder home became the main thoroughfare from Wickleberry to Settlers Cove. When they were offered a substantial amount of money to sell so the street could be widened, they took it and bought a new house in Wickleberry, this house. As a show of appreciation, the street was named after them, Fielder Street, which is still the best route over the hills.

In the late 1800s the lighthouse was built to help guide ships around the headland into the safety of the port. They were mostly tourist boats by this time. Then came cars and when US Route 1 linkage road was connected to Settlers

Avenue the trains stopped running and the line was closed. Settlers Cove boomed once again. More of Wickleberry was taken away when the forest was made a National Park. Wickleberry consisted of no more than a half dozen streets now and most of the houses were rundown. As the older generations of families died out, none of the younger generations wanted to live on this side of the hills. When the houses became too derelict, the Governor ordered their demolition and left the lots vacant. Today Wickleberry was viewed as a ghetto by those living in Settlers Cove. Jodie snapped back to herself and out of her memories. It made her feel connected knowing her family roots went right back to the beginning of her hometown but sad knowing what had become of her family.

Something under the edge of the mattress, next to the far wall caught her attention. She walked in and found it was Granny Jo's old leather herb pouch. Jodie picked it up and felt the soft leather with her fingers, surprisingly the drawstring was still attached, and she could see the floral pattern stamped into the soft leather. There were small holes at the center of the flowers, it was still lined with mesh; which stopped the herbs from escaping out the holes but not the smell. Granny Jo would make a mix of dried herbs and put them in this pouch and leave it under her pillow to give her good dreams. She made a mix a couple of times for Jodie after 'the accident' and Jodie remembered having nice dreams then too. It still held the smell of lavender and mint in its leather. She put it in her pocket and walked out of the room, closing the door behind her. She wanted to explore the rest of the house and see what else was still here.

She carefully made her way down the stairs. Some of the steps were soft underfoot if she got too close to the wall, so she stayed closer to the railing. She turned and went to the door under the stairs that led down to the basement and laundry. She opened the door, reached in and pulled the string. The light halfway down the stairs snapped on. She tested each step as she slowly made her way down to the bottom. She looked around in the dim light from above and the light coming in through the dirty easement windows and saw that there was broken furniture and boxes piled at the other end of the room. It was just then she realized for the first time that the basement didn't occupy the entire footprint of the house above. Funny how some things don't matter to you when you are young. She had been down here countless times with Granny Jo "helping" with the washing, although she was probably more underfoot than being any real help. With a sigh, she pulled the next string hanging down from the ceiling and the other light snapped on. She could see the washer and dryer were surprisingly still here. She doubted they still worked; they were almost dead when she had lived here. She passed them and walked to the pile of broken furniture and found the end of a wooden box. It looked a bit like a coffin. *What the hell is a coffin doing down here!*

Jodie cleared away some of the discarded trash, boxes and broken chairs off the top and found it was a coffin and it wasn't alone as there was another one. The other one looked older and was caked in dried black clay. *Black clay was found all through the hills,* Jodie thought as she took a step back and shook her head.

It can't be, Grandpa Don is buried up at Settlers Hill Cemetery and Crematorium. In that double plot that Granny Jo had been awarded after he'd been killed on the job, Jodie thought as she squeezed between the dirty coffin and the wall. She was looking for the small metal plaque that had been engraved and affixed to the lid of Grandpa Don's coffin. Jodie was having problems seeing in the dim lighting. She turned and went over to the easement windows. She used the end of her sleeve and wiped some of the grime off, to let more light in. She went back and felt the sharp edges of a small metal plaque. She brushed off the clay and leaned in close to read it. Engraved on the plaque was:

Donald Eugene Sargent
Born 1948 Died 2001

Jodie scrambled backwards away from the coffin in shock, tripped over something and landed hard on her ass.

She sat there staring at the coffins she knew, in the pit of her stomach, that the other one belonged to Granny Jo. Still, she made herself go and find the engraved plaque to make sure.

Josephine Athena Sargent
(Nee Fielder)

Jodie did not bother to read the rest of it. In a daze, she walked back up the stairs and sat on the top step looking down into the basement. Trying to make sense of it all. *How were they here? They're buried in that double plot awarded to them all those years ago,* Jodie thought, shaking her head. She stood and flipped the switch outside of the door and both lights in the basement went off. You could turn them both off with the switch at the top, but you had to pull the strings to turn them on. Grandpa Don had wired it up himself. Those memories were irrelevant. Why were their coffins in the basement? Other memories rushed at her from everywhere she looked as she slowly wandered away from the basement doorway. Like the dent in the wall from when she rode her bike inside and didn't make the corner, or where she had fallen and knocked a tooth out or the marks left where there used to be a door. She needed to get out of the house, she almost tripped over her feet they felt heavy and wouldn't move fast enough for her. She unlocked the back door with shaking hands and went out. She only stopped long enough to lock it behind her. She hoped the coffins were empty, but she knew in her heart they were not. That was when she started to run.

She didn't care who saw her run from the house, she didn't care which way she ran. She just ran trying to outrun her thoughts and memories. They swirled around inside her head and then slammed into her brain time and time again. The memories of growing up here were mostly happy and loving, others lonely, she didn't know where the last one came from. She couldn't remember ever being lonely in that house.

She tripped over the edge of a gutter, fell and landed sprawled out on a graveled sidewalk. She lay there face down and gasped for air like a beached fish. She rolled over and looked up at the sky as she tried to catch her breath. She propped herself up on her elbows and looked around trying to figure out where she was. She saw a sign behind her.

Settlers Hill Cemetery and Crematorium.

Slowly she stood up, brushed the dirt off herself as she walked towards the open gates. She wandered over to the information hut. The plot allocation list was mounted on the front wall. She hopefully searched for the Sargent double plot. The door to the hut opened and an old thin man walked out, stopped and looked at Jodie.

'Can I help you?' he asked.

'Yes, I'm trying to find my grandparent's double plot. Their last name was Sargent' Jodie answered, hoping this was a groundsman and not some guy squatting in the information hut.

He peered at her from under his bushy eyebrows as he scratched his gray beard. He stopped, leaned in close to her, standing over her. She could smell his sour breath; it made her uncomfortable with him being that close to her.

'The Sargent plot was reallocated, years back now. Wendy Fielder, the legal owner, sold it. I remember digging up the coffin that was already in there and putting it on the back of the flatbed truck, along with the other one. It was the saddest thing watching them being driven away'…

Chapter 4

Jodie sat on the floor of the mudroom, with her back against the back door. She had her knees drawn up to her chest and hugged them to herself. She felt dazed and wasn't sure how she had gotten home.

She had been right in her heart of hearts that Granny Jo and Grandpa Don were in the basement in their coffins. Her parent's ashes were in a glass mason jar in her rucksack. This place was her family's mausoleum. Her home, the only place where she ever felt she belonged, had been used as a dumping ground for the dead, and yet she still felt like she belonged here. Here amongst the dead, they were still her family.

Wendy's to blame for all of this, Jodie knew it. She had blocked Grandpa Don from being laid to rest in the Fielder Mausoleum, because he didn't have a Fielder last name. Granny Jo at least should have been left to rest in peace with her father. *Wendy had disowned her own half-sister, and the rest of the family tree which ended with me.*

Ψ

A voice whispered in the back of Jodie's mind: *'Maybe, it's time to disown her.'* As Jodie stood up, she whispered to herself 'It's time to visit Great Aunt Wendy' in a strange voice. Her face was blank, devoid of all emotion, her blue eyes looked like chips of ice and she moved with a sense of purpose. She walked from the backdoor into the kitchen looking for a knife and her stomach rumbled.

Ψ

She stopped, blinked, and her eyes returned to normal. She went into the pantry, climbed up the first shelf and felt around on the top shelf. She found the old can opener that was always up there. She picked up a can, looked at it and smiled. Baked beans never go off. She really wanted to eat, but she also realized that she stank. She smelt of sweat, blood and cigarettes. She felt she needed to wash and change her clothes. It was time to take her blood splattered jeans off.

She put the can and opener down on the bench and looked longingly at it, as she turned then walked down the hallway to the stairs. She touched the closed door to the basement as she passed and said, 'Love you both.'

****

Once she was back in her room she reached into her rucksack and pulled out the mason jar, carefully put it down beside her mattress. Then she knelt on the edge of her mattress as she upended her bag on it. Jodie realized she didn't have her cell phone, *not that I have anyone to call*. She put this thought out of her mind and continued to look for cleaner clothes. She found some socks; they didn't match but that didn't matter. She could feel the ones on her feet inside of her shoes were stiff from dried sweat. They needed to be changed. She found a pair of faded black jeans, they had been Lilian's, she wasn't much taller, she would only need to roll the cuffs up a couple of times, but they would fit. She found another pair of knickers. She never bothered with a bra, *you needed boobs for one of those and I don't have any*. She wore a singlet top instead; she found a black one and put that aside with the other clothes. She pulled out a faded purple hoodie from the pile. It had been Peg's. Jodie looked at it and as much as it wasn't really her thing, it was better than what she was currently wearing as it was clean. She didn't worry about a t-shirt as she would be wearing the singlet top. Even though it was summer now, it wasn't particularly warm inside the house, it was quite cold in here. Most summers she felt like she was going to sweat to death, as she didn't really feel the cold, except for when it was cold enough for sleet to pummel the coast. She picked up the pile of clothes as she stood up and walked to the bathroom.

She walked in and put her clothes on the closed toilet lid. Out of habit she closed the bathroom door, even though she was the only living person there. Then turned her attention to the small linen cupboard Grandpa Don had built into the wall near the door. It gave easy access to the pipes and some storage. You could only open it by pushing against it, there wasn't a handle on the outside.

Jodie pushed against it now and hoped no one had found it. She held the door open and whistled stunned by the cache of linen she found. There were towels, washcloths, sheets, pillowcases and even a few of the light waffle blankets. *Cool, I'll be able to make up my mattress.* She didn't see any pillows, but that didn't matter. She could stuff the pillowcases with a couple of towels. Right now, she wanted a towel and a washcloth, she took these out and pushed the door closed again.

Jodie bent down and looked in the cupboard under the vanity and found the plug. She was about to put it in the handbasin, then thought better of it, she remembered the brown water that came out of the tap in the kitchen. She turned on the hot tap and sure enough it was brown. She let it run, until it ran clear, but it didn't get any warmer. She put the plug in and filled it. Jodie knew her luck had to run out at some stage. The gas had been shut off to the property. Being able to wash was enough of a luxury.

She opened the mirrored cabinet and took out the new soap. Unwrapped it and left the wrapper on the vanity, she would throw that out later. She turned off the tap, soaped up the washcloth and washed her face, neck and head. Her black hair was getting longer, it was almost long enough to be grabbed and she didn't like that. She would need another shave soon. She liked having her head shaved. It was how head lice were kept under control in the Group Homes. Most saw it as some sort of punishment, but Jodie saw it as practical. She stripped off her clothes and shoes, laid her clothes over the edge of the tub behind her. She soaped up her chest, arms and as much of her back as she could reach and then rinsed it off with the washcloth. She repeated the process of soaping up and rinsing off the rest of her body. She only stopped soaping and rinsing when her skin started to tingle and became blotchy and red.

She dried herself with the towel and got dressed in the clean clothes, leaving the hoodie on the toilet lid so it wouldn't get wet. She pulled the plug, turned on the tap in the tub, when it ran clear she put the plug in. She needed only enough water in the bottom to cover her clothes. She pushed all her clothes into the tub and turned off the tap. Should she go see if the washer still worked? No, she wasn't ready to go back down to the basement just yet.

She hung the towel on the rack. She got busy soaping, scrubbing, and rinsing the clothes until, when she wrung them, the water that came out was clear of suds and dirt. She reached up and hung each piece over the shower curtain rod. The curtain was missing but that didn't matter. When she was finished, she pulled the plug and let the water out. Jodie used the tub to help push herself upright. She picked up the hoodie and put it on and then pushed the cupboard door open again. *May as well make my bed and get some of the housework done.* Her stomach twisted sharply and made her double over in pain. She should really have eaten already but she took a few deep breaths and made herself stand straight up again and continued with what she was doing.

She collected what she needed to make her bed, it smelled a bit musty and surprisingly not like rat pee. She walked back into her room and thought *it's so unusual not to find some sort of rat or mouse infestation in an abandoned place like this.* Then she remembered the coffins in the basement. *Why would they come up here when there was food and shelter down there?* That thought made her shudder. She shook her head trying to shake the thought out, it didn't really work, it just made her feel dizzy. To distract herself, she concentrated on making up her mattress.

She took one more look at her room before she closed the door. It was time to eat. She leaned into the bathroom and grabbed the soap wrapper off the edge of the vanity as she walked past. She made sure to walk on the rail side of the stairs as she almost skipped down the steps. She walked into the kitchen, leaned into the pantry and pulled out the small bin under the bottom shelf and dropped in the wrapper. She was surprised it was still here, so much of her usual was still in the house. She grabbed the can of beans and soon had it opened with the can opener then realized she didn't have anything to eat with. She was about to use her fingers when she decided to have a look in the drawer. She opened the top kitchen drawer, the cutlery divider was still there, full, and pulled out a spoon.

Jodie hopped up and sat on the kitchen bench and spooned her long-awaited food into her drooling mouth. She tried not to scoff it all in one go but it was so hard, she was so hungry. Too soon the spoon struck the bottom of the can, she looked in and chased the last of the beans around onto the spoon and ate them.

She rinsed the can out, before putting it in the bin. The rats may not have found a reason to be up here, and she didn't want to give them one either. While she was in the pantry she reached up and pulled all the cans down to her level and looked at what she had. There were pineapple pieces, baby beets, lima beans, more baked beans and a can of Irish stew. The Irish stew was out of date by a good couple of years as was thankfully the lima beans. She put those in the bin. She should really do a shop; she had some money. She wondered how long she could squat here in her old home. If she was careful who really knew how long she could stay here, her family was here, and she didn't really want to be anywhere else.

She turned and quickly ran upstairs to get some money. She was about to head out when she thought she should take some sort of bag with her. She opened the top cupboard in the mudroom, reached in and felt one of the canvas shopping bags and pulled it out. Looking at it made her laugh and think *damn it was good to be home.* She shoved the bag into her back pocket and made sure the cash was secure in her front pocket then unlocked the backdoor and went out.

Chapter 5

She had just locked the back door and was
walking towards the side gate, when it swung
open. She froze, trying to decide where there
was enough cover for her to jump behind. She
stood there staring at an old black man who was
standing in the gateway staring back at her. Jodie
wondered if she could charge past him, but all her
stuff was inside.

'Oh, it's you. It is you. Jodie, isn't it?' The old
man asked

Jodie looked at him. He kind of looked like
Max who lived over the back fence when she had
been little, except his hair had gone white. 'Max?'
she asked.

He nodded and said 'Yes. It looks like you've
come home. I'd noticed that the curtains in one
of the rooms upstairs had closed and thought
perhaps there were squatters here. I was just
coming around to chase 'em off.'

She didn't know what to do or say. He had

44

gotten old and had started to stoop. She had no idea how he was still alive.

It had gone quiet between them, so Max continued 'I know I don't look the same from when you used to live here but I'm still the same Max. I'm 75 now, you must be almost 21, if my memory still works.'

'Yes, I turn 21 in a few days, sorry, it's just been so long. I can't believe that the place is still standing and that you're still here' Jodie said, grasping for something to say.

Max closed the gate behind him and came closer and said 'What that Wendy bitch did to you was a cunt act. I did everything I could to stop the redevelopment. They wanted both these houses so they could have this entire small block for their new housing. I wouldn't sell, they even tried going around me and get my son to sell it to them but the Title is in my name so I said to them that they could have it after I turned up my toes and died, but they didn't want to wait for that. Then the Governor found out what they planned to build here, and they didn't have proper approval. They buggered off and left your Granny Jo's place to rot.'

Jodie looked down towards where the basement was and knew it wasn't the only thing left here to rot. She looked at Max and said 'Wow, 75, holy cow. Are you gonna chase me off?'

'Nah, you belong here, this is your home. I'll let the others keepin' watch know you are back here. They won't put you out either, this is your home. It should have gone to you, not that uppity bitch Wendy!'

Hearing him say that made her smile.

'Hey, you were headin' out...'

'Yeah, I'm going to do some shopping, can't live on old baked beans alone...'

'Oh, I won't hold you up, it's a bit of a walk over the hills to the shops.' He moved and opened the gate and walked out, she followed him and closed the gate behind her. Max turned back towards his house then turned and waved at her as she walked the other way heading towards the hills.

****

Hearing Max speak about Wendy like that brought back the memories from when she had to live with her. Jodie took off the hoodie and tied it around her waist, the memories consumed her as she walked over the hills to the shops.

Jodie was made to cook and clean Wendy's house. She could only have Wendy's scraps to eat. One day Jodie had taken some jewelry with the idea of selling it and running away. Wendy soon discovered she was missing some jewelry. Once Jodie realized Wendy had noticed the missing jewelry, she hid. Wendy found where Jodie was hiding and dragged her out. Jodie was unable to get any traction on the highly polished floor. Wendy screamed at her for being such an ungrateful and useless little bitch. She had taken her in when she had nowhere else to go. Jodie somehow managed to twist out of her grip. Wendy grabbed Jodie by the wrist before she could get away and that was when Wendy started to hit her. Jodie could never remember how many times she was hit, only that it had left her ears ringing. Wendy's many rings left bruises and deep cuts on Jodie who laid limp and bloody on the floor unable to even sit up. That was when Wendy grabbed her by the hair and dragged her over to the stairs and threatened to throw her into the small dark room underneath, if she didn't tell her where the jewelry was. Jodie could still remember looking into that dark void thinking that she had seen something reach for her. It had scared her more than Wendy right then and that was when she ran from it. Wendy had been left holding a clump of her hair, she didn't get very far before Wendy was on her again. She slapped Jodie hard across the face which knocked her to the floor, it left a painful imprint on her face that took several days to fade. She was being dragged back to the small dark room under the stairs.

That was when she told Wendy where she had hidden the jewelry. Jodie had to show her and when Wendy had the jewelry again, she locked Jodie in the attic as punishment.

Jodie was glad it wasn't that scary small dark room but it was summer and she felt like she was going to die in the sweltering heat of the attic. She knew screaming and banging to be let out would be a waste of time. She spent the time instead looking through the boxes stored there. After moving a few she had found a small decorative grate that let some light and air in. She used a plastic Christmas themed drink pitcher to collect her pee on the first day and drank it. Jodie had hoped that Wendy would give her something to eat or drink that night but she knew it was a false hope. The heat hadn't let up much during the night, she laid on the bare wooden floor with her face close to the grate breathing in the cooler air. By midmorning the next day, she hadn't peed again. She sucked the sweat from her clothes and licked it from her arms and legs. It tasted worse than her pee but it helped slacken her thirst and keep some moisture in her mouth. Her head ached and every time she sat up she felt dizzy. She spent most of the day laying down and only moved when she had to. By the end of that day, she was let out. Her body had felt like it was made of lead as she tried to get up off the floor. Wendy left the door open, walked away and left Jodie to get herself out of the attic. She gave up trying to stand and crawled out then fell down the small flight of stairs that led up to the attic. She landed in the main hallway of the house. She remembered how she lay there looking up at the ceiling enjoying the coolness. She knew she had come close to death. Jodie waited for her breathing and heart rate to decrease before she pulled herself along the hallway runner to her room. Wendy left her alone in her room for a few days. Jodie drank water from the sink in her connected half bath and ate her stash of cookies. Her recovery was taking too long for Wendy. When Jodie could walk again Wendy put her back to work. That was when Jodie knew she would have to fight to get out. When her full health had returned, she pushed Wendy down the main staircase.

Chapter 6

Jodie walked out of the shop with her small bag of cans and boxes of food. There was enough to keep her fed for the next week or so. She hadn't brought all her cash with her; she had to budget. It also made her workout in her head what would work together as a meal and what wouldn't. She still had those candies and chocolates. She turned to walk back home, looked up and saw a fancy car go by, it looked a bit like the one Wendy used to drive...

Ψ

Jodie's face went blank, and her eyes were pale as ice. She whispered to herself in a strange voice 'Time to visit the bitch'.

Jodie started walking faster in the direction of Wendy's place, she shouldered her way through the crowd. She didn't stop to apologize and kept on walking. One guy put his hand on her shoulder to stop her. She turned and first looked at his hand and then at him. She didn't say anything. He saw the promise in her pale eyes. The promise of death if he didn't remove his hand. He pulled his hand back like he had been burnt and watched her walk away. He was glad he wouldn't be wherever she was heading.

Ψ

Jodie was sitting naked huddled in the tub. It was dark outside the frosted bathroom window. The bathroom was lit by light coming in through the half open door, the landing light was on. She wondered if she should turn it off in case someone saw it. She shook her head; she wasn't thinking straight. She was confused. She had gone shopping, hadn't she? Why was she now sitting here hugging her knees in the cold water; which was tinged a reddish-brown. Maybe all the rust wasn't out of the pipes yet? But that didn't explain why she was having another wash. The last thing she remembered was walking out of the shops with her shopping bag of goods. No, wait, that wasn't right. She had seen something and had decided to visit Wendy... It didn't explain why it was so late or why she was sitting in an ice-cold tub! She looked down at herself and she could see where she had scrubbed herself raw, could that be why the water was that color?

She looked out over the edge of the tub and saw her crumpled clothes, there was something red on the floor near them. She stood up, slipped and grabbed the edge of the tub before she fell. Jodie stepped out of the tub. The air was colder than the water. She dried herself with the towel then wrapped it around her. Nothing was making any sense. She left here to go shopping at about noon because the sun was directly overhead. Where did all the time go? It was only about a three-mile round trip to the shops and back. It should have only been two or three hours. What the hell happened! She picked up the hoodie and it was covered in blood. She looked down at herself, she knew that there was no way any of that blood was hers. Whose blood, was it? Her jeans were smeared with a bloody handprint and splatters of something. Then she saw her shopping bag in the corner behind the door and it was covered in blood. She went over and had a look inside. The boxes were crushed, a couple of the cans were dented, but surprisingly the blood hadn't seeped through the canvas bag. She wondered then, *did someone jump me, and I fought back?*

She didn't want to deal with any of it right now. She suddenly felt really tired and all she wanted was to go to bed. She went into her room wrapped in the towel, stuck her hand into her rucksack and felt around until she felt the soft cloth of the onesie to sleep in. She let the towel drop and got dressed into her onesie. She did manage to pick up the towel and throw it back into the bathroom. She really didn't want to go back in there tonight. Tomorrow, that would have to wait until tomorrow. Jodie sat on her bed, reached over for Granny Jo's leather pouch, and smelt it, enjoying the old lavender and mint. It felt lumpy. Jodie opened the drawstring and tipped the contents out. Teeth, damaged plastic teeth, about a half dozen sat in her palm. She had no idea where they had come from or how they had gotten in there. She tipped them back into the pouch and put it under her pillow. It was just another thing she would have to try and figure out in the morning.

Not long after her head hit the pillow she was in a deep sleep. She slept like someone exhausted from a day of hard work. It was dreamless until the early hours of the morning; then she started to dream.

Ψ

At first, the dream was nice enough. She walked briskly down a tree lined street. It was late afternoon, it looked kind of familiar. There was a nice cooling breeze. She saw people staring at her, she slowed her pace. She even stopped to smell some flowers that were hanging over a low wooden fence. They had a delightfully sweet smell and were an assortment of gorgeous colors. Then she remembered Wendy lived on a street like this one, with its perfectly straight and evenly spaced trees. That was when it hit her. This was where Wendy lived, Settlers Avenue. She tried to change direction, but all too soon she had walked up the sidewalk and crossed the manicured lawn bordered by garden beds bursting with pretty flowers to Wendy's front door. She looked up at the imposing house. It was much too big for one person but there was no way Wendy would ever move into anything smaller. She tried to stop herself from lifting her hand, to stop herself from pressing the doorbell, but she couldn't.

Jodie saw a red nail polished hand come around the edge of the door like a claw as Wendy opened it. She was wearing her usual chunky gold rings on all her fingers. Jodie had to lean back to get any fresh air into her lungs, as Wendy's perfume hung around her like an invisible cloud of miasma.

She heard herself say nice and pleasant things, she saw Wendy smile and hold the door further open to let her in. She willingly walked inside, past the old bitch. Jodie walked to the center of the entry room and stood next to the highly polished walnut table. From here you could go to your left and into the front sitting room, straight ahead took you up the cream carpeted grand staircase to the next floor or if you turned right towards the archway; this took you into the formal dining room and then onto the kitchen through the swinging door. She turned when she heard the door close and the two deadbolts lock. Jodie took it all in, Wendy's gaudily printed dress, that was low cut in the front to show off her ample bosom and which she had just dropped the keys in. The dress sparkled where the sun reflected off the crystals sewn onto it. She wore golden sandals on her feet. Her permed hair fluffed into a golden halo around her head that seemed to glow in the sunlight coming through the glass side panels of the front door. The look was completed with heavy eye makeup and lipstick that matched her nail polish. Wendy was smiling at her like a cat does a mouse. Not that she was looking to eat her, more like she had trapped her plaything!

Jodie tossed and turned in her sleep, trying to wake herself up. She even tried to change what was happening. She held herself still in the dream, stopping herself from walking. Then she saw it. She saw her shadow walk out of her body and through the swinging door with Wendy. She was fascinated. She wondered if this dream was inspired by 'Peter Pan' because of Wendy's name. Jodie looked at the shadow but there wasn't anything playful about it, it felt wrong.

They were in the kitchen and Wendy was now instructing Shadow-Jodie on all the dos and don'ts if she wanted to live here again, Shadow-Jodie nodded in agreement. Wendy reached for the shopping bag in Shadow-Jodie's hand, but she held firm and wouldn't let go of it. Wendy tried shaking it loose and when that didn't work, she slapped Shadow-Jodie hard across the face, she stumbled back. Wendy let go of the bag, so it wouldn't pull her off balance as Shadow-Jodie fell.

Shadow-Jodie continued backwards but didn't fall, instead she crouched, twisted as she stood up and swung the bag around her until it collected Wendy in the side of the head. It knocked her over and she landed heavily on the marble tiled floor, leaving her stunned. Before she could cry out or get up, Shadow-Jodie swung the bag down onto Wendy again and again. Blood was flying everywhere. It sprayed across the floor, up the cabinets and onto the ceiling with every swing of the shopping bag. The bludgeoning didn't stop until the woman on the floor was silent and still. Shadow-Jodie stood over Wendy's bloodied broken body and swung the bag back down, one last time. It came down on Wendy's face with all her strength and Jodie heard Wendy's skull crunch from the impact!

Shadow-Jodie casually wiped the blood from her face with her hand and wiped it on her jeans. It wasn't over though, Shadow-Jodie dropped her bag and dragged Wendy from the kitchen to the top of the basement stairs, leaving a golden sandal behind in the trail of gore. The door was already open from when Wendy went around explaining things earlier. She watched Shadow-Jodie prop Wendy up at the top of the stairs and then kick her down them. They both followed. Shadow-Jodie laughed, there wasn't anything cheerful in the sound. Jodie giggled too when she saw how Wendy had landed at the bottom. What was left of her head was bent under her, her neck was clearly broken and her large rump in the air. Jodie watched Shadow-Jodie use her elbow to flick on the light switch. She then went over to the old Kelvinator fridge; it had been in Granny Jo's place while Jodie lived there. She was confused, why did Wendy have it? Why hadn't she gotten rid of it? It made no difference now, there was a use for it.

Shadow-Jodie emptied all the shelves out of the fridge. Jodie noticed Shadow-Jodie was using her hands in a funny way, then Jodie looked down and she had her sleeves pulled down over her own hands. Jodie understood then, Shadow-Jodie was using the ends of her sleeves to leave no new prints. Shadow-Jodie dropped the shelves down behind the chest freezer that was next to the old fridge. Jodie watched Shadow-Jodie fireman lift Wendy and cram her into the fridge. Shadow-Jodie slammed the door shut with her hip; its door threatened to reopen again. She stepped away and let it while she rummaged and found a snatch strap. She shimmed this down the back of the fridge and brought the ends together at the front. She shoved Wendy back into the fridge, stopped and pulled out what was left of her top false teeth, they came out in several pieces. She threw them down on the floor, smashing them, reached into Wendy's bosom and pulled out the keys. Jodie smiled seeing her once formidable Great Aunt Wendy's always perfect hair and makeup destroyed as much as her broken and bloody body, crammed into Granny Jo's old fridge. Shadow-Jodie then shoved her all the way into the fridge, closed the door and secured it with the snatch strap so it wouldn't open again.

Shadow-Jodie bent down and picked up the two front teeth, the two eye teeth and the two canines and put them in her pocket leaving the rest on the floor. She turned and walked back up the stairs and turned off the light at the top with her elbow. She closed the basement door with her foot. She didn't try to clean up the mess in the kitchen. She walked out into the hall and headed upstairs, leaving a trail of bloody footprints behind her. Jodie followed, intrigued. Halfway up the stairs the last of the blood rubbed off Shadow-Jodie's shoes. Jodie watched as Shadow-Jodie found and opened the safe with one of the keys she took off Wendy's body. She only removed the old jewelry boxes from the bottom and a couple of the bundles of cash. Shadow-Jodie opened the jewelry boxes to double check then closed and locked the safe again. Jodie recognized the boxes. They had belonged to Granny Jo's family. She followed Shadow-Jodie who calmly walked back downstairs, picked up her shopping bag, dropped the cash and jewelry into it, unlocked and walked out the back door. It surprised Jodie how dark it was outside. Shadow-Jodie closed the door but didn't lock it then walked through the back garden. She dropped the keys in the garden bed on her way past to open the gate and walked out onto the street. The sky was alive with fourth of July fireworks.

Ψ

Jodie was amused, shocked, horrified and sickened by what she had just dreamt but mostly pissed off. Wendy claimed all that jewelry had been stolen. She had even collected the insurance money!

Jodie stretched as she woke up and knew why she hurt so much. She had always been strong for her size, but just hadn't realized she could be that strong. She knew what she had to do today. She had some cleaning to do.

She pulled the leather pouch out from under her pillow, smiled, then rummaged around in her rucksack. She found a shoelace, *it would do*, tied it to the drawstring, made a loop and put it around her neck, stuffed the pouch down the front of her onesie.

Chapter 7

Jodie was hungry, but she also had some major cleaning to do and wondered if the clothes she washed yesterday were dry enough to wear today. She walked from her room and into the bathroom. *Yep, it was still a mess. Pity Shadow-Jodie couldn't clean up after herself.* This thought made her laugh. She carefully walked into the bathroom. The floor was still a little bit wet and she didn't want to slip and crack her skull open. Thinking of that now she could hear Wendy's skull crunch again, it just made her grin. She picked up the towel, which luckily had landed in a spot where the blood was dry. It looked like it had soaked into the grout. Jodie shrugged her shoulders and after hanging up the towel she walked out of the bathroom and back into her room.

She didn't want to risk getting any blood on her onesie, she took it off and put on a pair of knickers but didn't worry with a top, she'd soon work up a sweat. She walked back into the bathroom and pushed the cupboard door open and found cleaning products right down at the bottom. Everything was there, scrubbing brush, bucket, disinfectant, liquid soap and rags. She pulled it all out and put it on the edge of the vanity. Then she checked the clothes still hanging on the shower rod from yesterday and they were only touch damp. She left them where they were, she would wear them today, after she had cleaned the bathroom.

Jodie went over to her shopping bag, which was encrusted in blood, bits of bone and something else - probably brain goo. She tried to pick it up but it wouldn't budge, so instead held the bag open and removed her shopping from the bag piece by piece. She also took out the jewelry boxes and cash then stacked them in the corner between the toilet and the vanity cupboard, out of the way. She tried again to pick up the bag, it was stuck to the floor. She laughed as she wriggled and pulled at it until it came loose. She didn't want to damage it; *I'll need it again for more shopping.* It just needed to be washed. Finally, it let go of the floor and she chucked it in the tub. The tub still had water in it from last night, she didn't bother to drain it.

She scooped up her clothes from the floor and chucked them in the tub. She pulled her jeans out again, checked the pockets and found some change from her shopping. She put the change on the toilet lid, dropping her jeans back in the tub. The floor was clear and she stood up. Her back hurt, not surprising really considering what she hefted last night. The memory of how Wendy had landed at the bottom of the stairs made her smile. *Perhaps if I get something to eat and sort some of this other shit, my back will loosen up before I have to scrub these fuckin' floors and clothes.*

She pulled the almost dry singlet top down and put it on, then grabbed the gray jacket and used it as a sling to hold her food and other stuff. Jodie walked down to the kitchen. In the pantry she put the cans, most were a little dented, but none had burst, on the shelves. Jodie looked at the boxes and packets she had just dumped on a lower shelf. She opened the boxes and found only one had split the bag inside. Where the individual packets were intact, she binned the damaged boxes. She looked at the cans and tried to make up her mind about what to eat. She decided to just snack now, later though after cleaning, she would sit down and enjoy a meal. Jodie walked out of the pantry wondering when the trash bins were emptied. Could it still be the same night? She would have to find someone's trash bin to put her rubbish in at some point. For now, though, she had other things to deal with. She picked up the jacket with the jewelry boxes and cash and turned from the pantry, heading back upstairs.

She stopped at the threshold of the bathroom and groaned looking at the mess. She turned and walked into her room instead, put the jewelry in her bag then stopped and looked at the wad of cash in her hand. It made her grin in appreciation and this was only one of the two wads she had, there had been many more in the safe. She wouldn't need to sell Lillian's pills now. *Well, not for a very long time.* She put the cash in her bag, dropped the jacket on top and walked back to the bathroom. Time to get to work. Her stomach rumbled. Jodie went back to her room and pulled out a few of the candies, unwrapped them and shoved them all in her mouth. She walked from her room *no more procrastination time to get this shit done!*

****

It took longer than expected; getting the blood out of the grout had taken the longest. She noted to herself countless times while she scrubbed not to drop blood covered anything on the floor ever again. It belonged in the tub! The bathroom looked cleaner now than it did on her first day there. She looked at the washing hanging up hoping it wouldn't take long to dry. *Who knows when I might need another quick change of clothes?* Jodie frowned wondering where that thought came from. The last thing she did before walking out was get dressed and put the extra knickers back in her rucksack. *Now it's time for some fucking breakfast!*

Chapter 8

She enjoyed her well-earned breakfast, savored every mouthful, the only thing that could have made it better was if it had been heated and not congealed. After breakfast, she had a good look around her old house but was soon bored. The only thing of note she found was that the downstairs toilet was busted. The porcelain bowl was cracked, the floor and part of the wall had rotted away. You could now see into the study though the wall. Luckily this part of the house was on solid ground. She needed to turn off the water. Carefully she stepped in putting her feet on what looked solid and dry, using the walls for support so she wouldn't fall. The ground was green with slime and it smelt like an old swamp. She held her breath as she bent down, reached for and turned off the tap. She just made it back out the door before she passed out, she slammed the door shut behind her as she took a couple of deep breaths.

She opened the door to the basement and stood there looking into the grayness it held, questioning if she should go down or leave it, *yeah, another day, nope, now is good enough.* With her mind made up she pulled the string it was time to show some respect and get the rest of the rubbish off the coffins.

She pulled the other string at the bottom of the stairs. Then started to carefully remove the boxes that had been chucked on top of the coffins. Some were empty, others had broken bits of crockery or odds and ends in them. She found a box of old gardening magazines; they had been Granny Jo's, those she put near the stairs. Jodie made two piles, one near the old washer and dryer, for the shit. The other pile near the bottom of the stairs of stuff that could entertain her later, or be of use.

Jodie was starting to get tired when she heaved the last bit of shit off the coffins. Nothing was under them, which meant they had been deliberately buried under everything. Jodie turned to the boxes near the stairs and pulled out an old lace tablecloth, being careful not to drag it on the dirty concrete floor. She stopped, looked at the black clay on Grandpa Don's coffin, put the tablecloth back in the box and rummaged through a couple of boxes until she found something to clean the coffin with. The clay was so old and dry it flaked off easily, some turned to dust which made her sneeze, it didn't take long to clean. She straightened the coffins as best as she could, so Granny Jo and Grandpa Don lay side by side. She returned and collected the tablecloth then she covered them with it. She straightened it out and made sure there weren't any creases in it. She found an old stool that didn't wobble horribly and put that at the foot of the coffins. She ran back upstairs and collected the mason jar and jewelry boxes.

Jodie opened the smallest jewelry box, it contained both of her parents' white gold wedding bands. She put them in the jar. There was also a small bracelet in there too, Jodie's dad had bought this for her mom when they had found out she was pregnant. She left this in the box and put it next to the jar. She peeked into the larger jewelry boxes; they held the Fielder family heirlooms. There were large heavy pieces like Cameo Brooches and Widow Lockets. The Widow Lockets had a clear crystal insert in the back that you could see hair through and if you opened them, you saw a small hand painted miniature of the deceased husband. There were a couple of sets of cufflinks, one with large pretty green gems, the other set had the Fielder Family Crest on them, also some chunky necklaces and bracelets. These boxes she placed on the cloth covering the coffins.

Jodie turned her attention to the pile of shit near the washer. She decided to use this to make a dividing wall for the coffins and the rest of the basement. It took a bit of figuring out and once it was at her hip height she stopped. She didn't want it falling on the coffins. She stood back and admired her handiwork. She would have preferred that they were buried in the ground, but it looked better now.

Jodie picked up the box of gardening magazines before she went back upstairs. At the top she turned and said, 'Love you all', closed the door and flicked off the light with her elbow.

As she walked up the stairs to her room, she realized she would be 21 the day after tomorrow on the seventh.

Chapter 9

The next morning Jodie was sitting on the kitchen bench, eating the last of some sort of stew out of a can, when there were a couple of light knocks on the back door. Jodie put the can down and jumped off the bench and peeked out through the edge of the curtain over the window in the backdoor. Max standing there. She smiled and opened the door for him. That was when she saw the box at his feet.

'Good morning to the birthday girl' Max greeted her with a smile.

'Aww thanks' Jodie answered, he was a day early but she couldn't bring herself to correct him. Besides, it had been longer than she cared to remember anyone wishing her a "Happy Birthday".

'I've told all of 'em still here in the neighborhood, it's you livin' here, and they were happy you were back, some were even able to chip in for the birthday girl.' He said in a rush, with a huge grin on his face. He bent down and picked up the box and gave it to her.

Jodie investigated the box and saw an awesome assortment of stuff. She propped a corner of the box on the edge of the brick planter box at the side of the porch, to have a better look. She looked up and smiled at the still beaming Max and said 'Thanks so much for all of this. Just a question; when do the trash bins get emptied?'

Max was surprised by the question but realized of course she would have trash to go out and answered 'They changed it from when you lived here. It's now once every two weeks, although they gave us extra bins. As if that makes up for the smell of our rubbish rotting in our bins waitin' to be emptied. The next one is in a couple o' days, this Friday. I leave my trash bins just inside my back gate, it isn't locked. You're welcome to drop your rubbish there.'

'Thanks so much, with everything still here, I found it odd that the trash bins were gone.'

'People probably stole 'em 'cause you can have up to four bins for a house but only two are free. You have to pay to get the other two…'

'Typical' Jodie said with a small laugh. She turned her attention back to the box. She picked up a packet of four cupcakes.

'Those are from Harriet, across the road from me, she's almost as old as I am but much fitter.' Max said with a low whistle at the end, which made Jodie grin back at him.

Next, she pulled out a small saucepan and skillet, 'Oh those are from Rupert, he lives just around the corner from Harriet, lucky devil.'

Jodie reached in and pulled out a bag of gas cylinders, they had been tied to the small gas stove, 'That lot's from Margery and me, she's over the road from you on the corner of Hill Climb. She moved into the neighborhood about a year or two after you left. According to Harriet, Margery's husband had run off with some young floozy after he'd emptied their joint bank account, the bastard. She had to sell the house to pay off the mortgage on her old place. Which only left her with enough cash to buy another place on this side o' the hills.' Max filled in for Jodie when she looked confused as she didn't recognize Margery's name. He then continued 'I know you still have water and power, 'cause they never bothered to shut 'em off. You need something to cook with and boil water for bathin'. They did manage to shut off the gas, probably only 'cause it was a fire hazard if it leaked.'

Jodie didn't know what to say so she hugged Max awkwardly around the box. She wasn't a hugging person. He accepted her hug and hugged her back as hard as she hugged him. After a bit he gently pushed her away, there were tears in his eyes. He turned away and used the cuff of his cardigan to wipe his tears away. He turned back to her with a smile on his weathered old face and said 'I'm so glad you like it all, none of us have much. Vernon who still lives on the corner of Wickleberry Station Lane and Bayview Street and then there's old Syd on Norman Street wanted to chip in too, but they couldn't give you anythin' but they'll keep the secret that you're back home. We're all just hopin' for that Wendy bitch to drop dead, then maybe you'll inherit what was rightfully yours. We can only hope.' He said while still smiling.

He lifted his flat cap and bowed to Jodie and said as he straightened up again, 'Happy birthday beautiful girl' and walked away.

Jodie stood there and watched him leave; she waved goodbye to him as he closed the side gate before she went back inside. She was eyeing off those cupcakes, they looked delicious.

Chapter 10

Jodie put the box down on the kitchen bench. It was going to be so good not to eat congealed stew out of a can anymore. She took out the cupcakes. They were chocolate with little white sprinkles on top. She couldn't help herself and took one out of the molded plastic container, peeled the paper cup down and bit into it. It was moist, soft and so yummy. She shoved the rest of it in her mouth and enjoyed the sweetness.

As she chewed her cupcake, she took the skillet and small saucepan out and put them on the shelf under the kitchen bench. She took the gas stove and its cylinders to the pantry. There were four cylinders they would keep her going for a while. She didn't think she would use them for bathing. She was used to having cold washes, maybe during winter she would change her mind. She grabbed out another cupcake before picking up the empty box and took it to the mudroom. She would use it to take her garbage out. She saw a copy of The Cove Daily in the bottom, as she put the box on the floor.

Jodie picked it out and spread it out on the built-in bench seat in the mudroom to read it. Inside the front cover was a big article on a local couple being honored for their selfless lifelong work within the Foster Care system. They had only just retired and had been given a "Service to the Community Award".

She looked at the photo and dropped her second cupcake on the floor as her whole body went numb. The picture was of Bert and Dorothy Smythe standing in front of their house, *also known as "The Cabin in the Woods" by anyone like myself who's had the displeasure of staying there.*

They were older but she still recognized them. Bert had lost his hair and his beard had gone white. Jodie still recognized him by his squinty little eyes behind his glasses. Dorothy's hair had gone from dark brown to a steel gray. It was styled the same way as she remembered, in an elbow length plait hanging over her shoulder. Jodie had stayed with them after Wendy had gotten rid of her. She had been too young to go to a group home at that stage.

Jodie screwed up the newspaper and threw it across the room. She picked up her cupcake from the floor and shoved it into her mouth. She almost choked on it but she didn't care. She didn't want to remember! She needed something to get them out of her head. She turned and strode through the kitchen, grabbed the container holding the last two cupcakes and ran upstairs. She slammed her door closed and sat down with her back to it. Trying to keep those memories out of her head that were coming back. She had been too young to really stand up for herself back then.

She had endured so much in her life and it was all there just under the surface. As soon as anything disturbed the surface it all came bubbling up. Forgotten memories, memories deliberately buried or blotted out. She didn't want to face what others had made her see, hear, be a part of or had done to her. *Not now, not ever!*

Jodie was shaking and crying as she shoved another cupcake into her mouth. She inhaled and choked on her cupcake. She couldn't breathe. She stood up and started to shake herself bent over double. She coughed up the cupcake and it launched from her mouth.

Ψ

Shadow-Jodie whispered in the back of her mind *'Typical, can't have one happy day, just one'* It was the last thing Jodie heard before she passed out.

Ψ

Chapter 11

Jodie rolled over in bed; she couldn't remember going to bed. Not after... She didn't want to think about that, not now, not ever. Then she heard the garbage truck emptying bins in the street, and was confused.

Max had said that bins were emptied the day after tomorrow, which was Friday. She looked and saw what was left of the cupcake still on the floor where it landed after she had coughed it up.

She knew Max was old, but he wasn't silly; he had only been out with her birthday by one day. Her hand strayed to the pouch around her neck, as she moved the teeth around inside, it seemed fuller. She sat up and pulled it from her neck, peered into it and found it held more teeth. Real teeth and not just the plastic ones from Wendy.

'OH SHIT!' Jodie scrambled up out of bed to look in the bathroom. She was wearing her onesie, but she was worried about the mess in the bathroom. She had only just cleaned that up from last time!

She came around the corner and had to grip the edge of the doorway or she would have slipped on the wet tiles. All she saw were the clothes she had been wearing hanging up on the curtain rod drip drying, she peered into the tub and saw a bit of a high tide of dirt but no blood.

Jodie laughed and guessed that she could teach Shadow-Jodie. She had no doubt that was what had happened this time. She must have really wiped herself out doing it, because she didn't wake up again until now. Unlike last time when she was still in the tub. *This works, I wonder if I'll dream about it later or get flashbacks, either way's cool,* she was almost looking forward to seeing what Shadow-Jodie had done. She smiled and skipped down the stairs looking for something to eat for breakfast. She was famished.

Chapter 12

Jodie walked into the kitchen and saw the screwed-up newspaper on the floor. She picked it up, didn't bother to look at it but put it in the bin in the pantry. While she was in there, she got the gas stove and a cylinder off the shelf and carried them to the kitchen bench. She went back and looked at her selection of cans and decided on the spaghetti with meatballs. She put that on the kitchen bench next to the stove. She reached down to the shelf under the bench and pulled out the little saucepan. She then set about making breakfast.

While it was heating on the stove, she looked in the cupboards for something to eat out of. She was happy enough to eat out of the saucepan, but she still had a look. She squatted down and looked right to the back of the bottom shelf and found something looking back at her.

She froze, she didn't want rats in the place. After staring and being totally still for a little while she realized it wasn't moving. She shuffled herself sideways and it didn't move but that did let in more light. She let out the breath she didn't know she had been holding. Jodie giggled nervously, reached in and took a hold of the object and pulled it out. She had no idea how it had gotten in there; it was a Mr. Cubby teddy. He had been one of her toys when she was little, he was a small hard packed bear. He wasn't soft, but he had been handmade by someone for her. He had a little tool belt around his waist and a hardhat on his head.

Jodie was so engrossed in what she had found that when the hot sauce from her food splattered on her, she jumped and dropped him. She quickly turned the stove off and let her food sit to cool.

She bent down and picked him up off the floor. She smiled at him and then she had a shooting pain tear though her head and she managed to drop him on the kitchen bench and grabbed hold of the edge so she wouldn't fall over. She whispered to herself 'What the hell'. The pain was soon gone but it left her a little bit shaky. It took a few good deep breaths to steady herself. When she held her hand out in front of her eyes and saw that it had stopped shaking, that was when she pulled open the drawer and got a fork out. It was time for food.

She turned away from the stove with the saucepan in her hand and left Mr. Cubby on the kitchen bench where he had landed on his side. She walked out of the kitchen and into the mudroom and sat on the bench seat to eat. Jodie made sure she didn't put the still hot saucepan on her knees and held it away from herself. She stabbed a meatball with her fork and blew on it to cool it down before eating it. It was almost ambrosial after eating cold congealed food out of a can.

Jodie's mind strayed to the missing time and what may have occurred during it. She shook her head. She could think of that later, right now she wanted to know how Mr. Cubby was still here. How and why was he in the cupboard? He must have been chucked in there. If the rest of her toys had been good enough to take, why wasn't he? He had been handmade for her. She couldn't remember when she had gotten him, but she was only ten when Granny Jo had died. Jodie tried to remember playing with him but couldn't. It was blank, she knew better than to push, so many of her memories she had shut out, buried or deleted, it was safer that way. She couldn't understand why she would blank out memories about a toy though.

Jodie had another shooting pain rip through her brain, it caused her to drop the saucepan. The last of her food splattering across the floor. She reached up with both hands to her head to try and stop the pain. An image popped into her mind. It was of an ugly looking dark-haired guy with a crazy happy lopsided grin on his face and he was above her looking down on her. She squeezed her eyes shut trying to block the image, she held her breath concentrating on getting rid of his face. Finally, she passed out.

Ψ

Jodie had slid from the bench seat and was sprawled out on the floor; Shadow-Jodie was standing over her looking down at her and whispered *'Soon.'* Shadow-Jodie knelt beside Jodie and gently placed a shadow hand on Jodie's forehead and faded as she flowed into Jodie.

Ψ

Jodie mumbled and her head rolled from side to side. Eventually she blinked her eyes open. She couldn't understand why she was laying on the floor. She pushed herself up and sat up. She looked at where her food had landed 'Oh for fuck's sake' she said exasperated. With a groan she got up and walked into the kitchen. She didn't look at Mr. Cubby as she picked him up and opened the bottom cupboard, chucked him in and closed the door again. She cleaned up the mess and then packed away her stove. Walking out of the pantry she wondered what she should do with herself now and remembered the cupcake upstairs in her room. She looked around the kitchen but couldn't find the other cupcake. Jodie turned and walked down the hallway. She knew there had been four in the packet. She had eaten two and launched one across her room.

She walked into her room and looked at it. It looked so sad sitting there, she picked it up and went looking for the packet and the last one.

Ψ

Shadow-Jodie whispered in the back of her head *'Hiking rations.'* Jodie shook her head and said 'What?' She hadn't really expected a reply.

Ψ

She went back downstairs and put the now stale cupcake in the bin. She should really get dressed and take the bin out. Then she remembered that the garbage truck had already been though, 'ah fuck it' she said to herself.

Still, she should get dressed, her other set of clothes should be dry by now. She turned and headed for the bathroom.

Jodie stood at the bathroom threshold looking at the clothes dripping onto the floor. She shook her head. Shadow-Jodie may have cleaned up this time, but she still had a few things to learn. Jodie carefully entered; the floor was slippery. She pulled down her wet clothes from the shower curtain rod and threw them in the tub up the opposite end to the drain. She then picked up one piece at a time and wrung it out over the drain. Once that was done to her liking, she picked up the towel that was sitting on the toilet lid. She used this to mop up the water on the floor and hung the towel up to dry. She pulled the dry clothes down from the shower curtain rod and walked out of the bathroom. Time to get dressed.

****

Jodie couldn't stop herself. After getting dressed she pulled the leather pouch from around her neck. She poured the teeth into the palm of her hand. She now had three sets of six teeth. One lot were the damaged plastic set from Wendy, the other two sets were real. They had long roots; she could still see some blood and meat stuck to them. It made her smile as she slid them from her hand and back into the pouch. She looped it back around her neck, sat down on her bed leaning her back against the wall and said, 'I'm ready, show me'. She thought to herself *I've nothing else to do today, time to find out where the last two days went.*

Chapter 13

Ψ

She heard a faint laugh and then she was there. She was walking along beside her Shadow-self on the side of a road. She had no idea where they were going. Nothing they passed looked immediately familiar to her. She could see where the last cupcake went, her Shadow-self ate it. They seemed to walk for a long time in the dappled shade cast from the big trees they passed. Jodie guessed they were walking along Gorge Grove that went through the National Park. She spied the sun through the trees. It was starting to get low in the sky. As they passed a signpost, they turned up a narrow lane. They had left Gorge Grove onto Spruce Lane. Spruce Lane, the name alone made her want to turn and run home. She had been so young and scared the last time she was out here and she didn't want to be here now. She stumbled on the uneven dirt as she remembered her history tied to this place. She tried to distract herself with some of the local history of Wickleberry. It had been expanding, several families had bought land along Gorge Grove. Then National Parks took hold of the old growth forest, and all but one property was bought back.

Then she saw it. The only house still out there. It had been left as it had been the first house built so it was part of the cultural heritage of the area. She watched her Shadow-self walk into the trees surrounding the house, she reluctantly followed.

Jodie didn't want to go in there. She was being bombarded with memories, horrible memories of this place. Dorothy was a mean person. She would kick over the suds bucket while you were trying to scrub the floor. Then you had to clean that up too. If it wasn't done before Bert noticed, then he would take you into the study and close the door. If you were lucky, he only beat you. Jodie had been lucky and she knew it. She was lucky for a couple of reasons; she was a white girl and a local.

Jodie was never any good at making friends, but she did make one here, Lucy. They had shared the bottom bunk, as neither of them were particularly big, so it was plenty big enough for them both. Lucy had been a cheerful Latino girl, convinced that she would soon be collected by her Grammy, once she found out where Lucy had been taken. Lucy had been one of those girls who lit up a room when they walked into it. People were drawn to her - Bert was one of them. Lucy never told what he did to her, but Jodie had seen the blood on the sheets of their shared bed.

One day Jodie woke up and Lucy was gone. Dorothy said Lucy had run away into the woods after Bert had disciplined her again. Jodie never saw Lucy again. Lucy was only one of a long line of girls and boys who had run away. Bert and Dorothy never went looking for them and they never bothered telling the authorities. They both said it was because if the authorities knew that they couldn't contain the kids then they wouldn't get anymore. If Jodie wanted to sleep on the stone floor, then go ahead and tell the authorities. They would lose their funding, and no one wanted her. The authorities would leave her with them! She was told so many times there were worse places than staying with them and Jodie had believed them for a while. Then one day Dorothy pushed her and she landed awkwardly, it hurt. When Dorothy laughed, that was when Jodie hit her. Next thing Jodie knew she was being bounced to the next place.

The memories faded and it was night time with only the moonlight peeking through the trees. Jodie followed Shadow-self as she walked towards the house. She saw that the side steps of the house were being rebuilt. It looked like Bert had already built the brick foundation. Next to it there were bags of cement and cement boards piled up. He had already framed the slab ready to be poured. That usually was the front door, they walked past it and went around back. Jodie saw Shadow-self collect and put on the gardening gloves that always hung by the backdoor.

Jodie watched as Shadow-self turned the handle. She knew the back door was usually unlocked. It swung open, Shadow-self walked in and Jodie followed into the sunroom with a stone floor. It had been a veranda at one point then it had been built in. She saw Dorothy stop part way across the kitchen, with a big bowl of soup in her hands. She screamed, but Jodie didn't hear it and only saw her gaping mouth. Shadow-self grabbed the shovel which was kept just inside the back door. Bert came charging in from the study, Shadow-self swung the shovel hard at the oncoming Bert. The flat back of the shovel smashed into the side of his head with a ringing crunch and knocked him to the floor. Jodie watched as his glasses flew off his head, it was almost like it was in slow motion as they sailed away from him, before they smashed on the stone floor where they landed. Dorothy threw her pot of hot soup in their direction screaming. Shadow-self dodged the soup easily and smacked her down with the shovel.

Shadow-self quickly grabbed the roasting string off the kitchen bench, taking advantage of the incapacitated couple. Jodie watched as they were tied up with the string. Once restrained, Shadow-self went back to the kitchen. There she collected a meat tenderizer and also a small set of pliers from the junk drawer. She sat first Bert and then Dorothy up against the wall of the sunroom. Jodie looked at Dorothy, she had a huge swelling on her forehead. Jodie could hear her now; she was blubbering, offering all the money and anything of value in the house. Alternating the blubbering with yelling that the authorities would get her and lock her up for what she was doing. Then she screamed that she always knew Jodie was scum, that was when Shadow-self slammed the tenderizer into Dorothy's face. It smashed her nose which caused blood to spurt out hitting them all, then it dribbled down Dorothy's chin and onto her moss-colored cable knit jumper. She still made choking noises but wasn't talking anymore.

Shadow-self turned to Bert, he had blood oozing from his ear, down his neck and onto his dark blue cardigan. His eyeball had popped out of its socket and it rolled back and forth on his cheek as he screamed at her. Jodie could hear him clearly now that Dorothy had shut up. He screamed about her being their only failure because they couldn't just say she had run away. They always told the authorities eventually and said that they hadn't wanted to report the runaways hoping that they would come back. He knew that because they had been ethnic minorities or some other undocumented citizen no one would really look for them. Jodie had been the only real blemish on their record and what she was doing now just proved that she was scum.

That was the last thing he said to her. Shadow-self picked up the shovel from where it had been dropped. Then she used her full strength and drove the length of the shovel's blade through his neck until it hit the wall behind him and splintered the wood. When she pulled the shovel back a double spray of blood from his severed jugulars hit Dorothy and the floor. Bert's head rolled off the shovel onto his legs and then the floor next to him. It left a trail of blood down his cardigan and across his jeans. Dorothy watched in silent horror as her husband's decapitated head rolled to a stop near her foot, his eye still open. Dorothy started to blubber again. She choked out that it was all because of Bert. He couldn't keep his hands to himself, he got the young girls knocked up or he was too rough with the little boys. She looked after them all, they were all her Angels now. Shadow-self brought the flat back of the shovel down hard on the top of Dorothy's head. This shortened her neck and her head now sat between her collar bones. More blood flowed out her nose and mouth and it followed the path down her chin and onto the front of her jumper. What didn't seep into her yellow apron pooled in her lap. She continued to make gurgling noises.

Shadow-self turned away and went to the still open back door and looked out at the fenced herb garden. It was Dorothy's pride and joy. It was decorated with Angel statues. Jodie watched Shadow-self trying to decide what to do next. Shadow-self carried the shovel with her as she went outside and walked along the small well-worn path to Dorothy's garden. She left the shovel by the gate.

Shadow-self walked around the house to the completed foundation of the side steps. She looked up at the near full moon directly overhead, then walked inside through the back door, Jodie followed. Shadow-self walked through the wet blood, leaving bloody footprints behind. She unlocked the side door and threw it open. She dragged Dorothy across the floor first, leaving a trail of blood behind to the open side door, she was still making a few odd noises. Shadow-self walked back and collected the tenderizer from where it had been dropped and used it to smash in Dorothy's face. Her face caved in from only two hits. The sound was odd, Jodie had been bracing for a cracking or crunching noise like Wendy's head made, but instead there was only a sloppy smoosh. It amazed Jodie how far the blood flew off the tenderizer and up onto the ceiling, she looked at it and realized that there was more than just blood up there. Dorothy's face must have already been badly fractured from the first blow with the tenderizer and then from the shovel coming down on top of her head. Shadow-self dropped the tenderizer satisfied that she didn't need the pliers. She stuck her hand into the mess that had been Dorothy's face, searching she pulled out several pieces of bone and other teeth and dropped them on Dorthey's chest. Shadow-self only stopped when she had the teeth she wanted. These she put in her pocket. Then she shoved Dorothy out of the door and into the foundations. Jodie peered out at her and laughed as she watched the crotch of Dorothy's jeans darken as she pissed herself.

Bert wasn't tall, but he was surprisingly heavy, even without his head. Shadow-self rolled him across the floor. He left an odd pattern of red and brown, Jodie giggled when she realized that Bert had shit himself. *I'm glad that I can't smell it* Jodie thought. Before Bert was pushed out, Shadow-self walked back and collected his head and the pliers. She put his head between her feet, she looked over at the tenderizer, took a step towards it and stepped onto his eyeball that had fallen out of its socket. It was squashed under her shoe and as she twisted on her toe it was ground into the floor when she changed her mind. Instead, she gripped his head between her feet as she pulled his six front teeth with the pliers and put them in her pocket. Then chucked his head out the door. It landed in the foundations between Dorothy's legs. That made Jodie giggle and Shadow-self laughed, it wasn't a pleasant sound. Shadow-self lifted Bert's legs so he would fit through the doorway sideways and rolled him out the door and into the hole. He landed heavily on Dorothy; Jodie heard Dorothy's ribs crunch as they broke under his weight. His momentum rolled him off her. Shadow-self closed and locked the side door.

Shadow-self went out the back door and got to work, there wasn't much left to do to finish the stairs. Jodie watched with fascination as Shadow-self put the cross beams inside of the wooden edging. Then covered them with the cement boards and mixed the quick set cement, poured it and smoothed it out a couple of times. She left the form in place as the cement still had to harden. It might not have been a lot to do but it took time. The sky had started to get light as Shadow-self smoothed the cement one last time. She packed the rest of the cement bags and assorted materials away in the shed.

Shadow-self walked over to the house, went inside and closed the back door behind her. She went over to the couch and fell onto it. She hadn't bothered to take her shoes off and bits of blood, bone and dirt that caked the soles of her shoes fell off. Jodie had always found that old black couch uncomfortable to lay on as the springs were shot and they poked through the worn corduroy cover but she guessed that Shadow-self was too tired to care. It was good this house was so isolated. It was at the end of Spruce Lane and the only house on it. Bert's family owned all the land from where Spruce Lane left Gorge Grove, the only road through the National Park. Back when Jodie was staying here that isolation worked for Bert and Dorothy. Now it worked against them. They had been happy being alone together, everyone knew they were never social people. The chances that anyone would visit were so low, it had been a risk worth taking to get some shut eye.

Jodie felt odd watching her Shadow-self sleep. Then it was getting dark again, which didn't mean that it was late. The tall trees around the house would start to block the sun by 2pm. Shadow-self sat up and stretched. Jodie heard her back crack a few times before Shadow-self climbed off the couch. She went over to the kitchen sink, turned on the tap, took off the gloves, splashed some cold water on her face, roughly rinsed it, put the gloves back on and turned off the tap. Shadow-self turned, looked at the mess and laughed as she walked through the still sticky mess to pick up the pliers from the floor. Then used them to gouge ruts in the long timber table from one end to the other. It was made from a single slab of wood by one of Bert's long dead relatives several generations ago, you could easily seat eight people and still have room to spare. It was decorated with carvings of local flora up its legs and along the edges of the tabletop. Jodie had been made to gently sand and polish that very tabletop more than once. It was Bert's pride and joy. He always supervised her when she was made to work on it and if she messed it up, he would punish her. Now it sported some long ugly gouge marks. Shadow-self dropped the pliers, laughed at the damage done to the table and walked out the back door, making sure it was closed properly behind her.

Shadow-self walked to Dorothy's herb garden; she had always been so proud of how abundant it was. She used to do a seasonal drying of her herbs in the shed. Then she would meet up with others in the area to swap her little bunches of herbs for some she didn't grow. Dorothy loved to cook and she would never use bought herbs.

Shadow-self grabbed the shovel as she pushed the gate open, then walked to the far corner where one of the larger angels stood. There was a collection of Angels and Fairies placed around the herb garden. Jodie understood now what they meant, Angels for young lives taken. The Fairies represented the children never to be born. It made her angry. Shadow-self started to dig. She dug until she hit something hard. Jodie watched as Shadow-self dropped the shovel and then sat down and dug by hand, she carefully removed the dark rich soil one handful at a time. Soon she was smoothing the dirt off something, it was round, finally Jodie saw and recognized the shape of a human skull. Once enough of it was exposed so you could clearly see what it was, Shadow-self stopped, stood up and brushed the soil off herself.

Jodie watched as Shadow-self picked up the shovel then thrust it deep into the ground near the exposed skull and walked from the herb garden. Jodie walked with Shadow-self past the finished side steps, down Spruce Lane and headed for home. At Jodie's street, the trash bins were out. Shadow-self stopped at one and peeled off the gardening gloves and dropped them inside.

Ψ

That was the last thing Jodie saw before she opened her eyes again. She was sitting in her darkened bedroom. Jodie blinked into the gathering gloom. It took most of today for her to see where she had been for two days. No wonder she had been so hungry and she was hungry again too. She stood up and stretched and looked at her clothes, she got changed back into her onesie. She shouldn't have bothered getting dressed today.

She walked down to the kitchen, looked in the direction to where Mr. Cubby was in the cupboard, but she couldn't make herself walk over there. She went to the pantry instead and got a bag of crushed cookies down off the shelf. It was all she felt like having. They had been on special when she bought them, but Wendy's head had destroyed the box and crushed the cookies. She took her cookies back to her room. She was suddenly tired and wanted to snack and then sleep.

Chapter 14

Jodie spent the next week catching up with Max and the others who still lived in the neighborhood. She helped Max with his gardening. He had a good-sized vegie patch and what he couldn't eat he happily shared. It was nice to be outside in the dappled sunshine under the big old Weeping Willow that grew in her backyard and hung over their dividing fence. She remembered climbing it when she was small and talking to Max and his family when they were in their backyard. He had told her, all those years ago, when she had asked why there were only two houses back-to-back on their block.

There had been a small walking park on this block for new moms. It had been built so they could get some fresh air while having a short stroll with their newborn bubs. There were a few benches and a small fountain in the middle of manicured garden beds. It had a wrought iron fence around it and gates. It was only unlocked and open for visiting at respectable hours and never at night. Then Wickleberry had boomed, and more space was needed to build on. The garden was bulldozed and their two houses were built back-to-back.

Spending time outside with someone made her feel like she was part of the world. She went shopping with him. She had offered to go for him as it was such a long walk but he had laughed, thanked her and said it kept him fit. When they got back, he cooked and fed her to thank her for keeping him company.

She spent some time with Rupert who was nice. Granny Jo used to say he reminded her of Robert Redford. He had so many beautiful paintings and sculptures of men in his home. Jodie realized that Max had nothing to worry about. Rupert wasn't into women; Harriet was safe living next to him. Although Max might have to worry if Rupert turned his gaze towards him instead. It made her laugh that all these oldies were acting much younger than their years would indicate. Her neighbors were all well past middle age, most were into their 70s.

Rupert pointed out an article in his current copy of The Cove Daily. It was about a local guy being awarded a grant to build cubby and tree houses. Rupert wasn't supportive and said it was a waste of money. Jodie had asked for the newspaper. She didn't know why but she suddenly wanted it when she had heard the name "Lonny". Rupert had already read it so happily gave it to her.

Jodie walked home with the newspaper in her hand. Not knowing why she had to have it. She still had plenty of things to read.

Chapter 15

As soon as Jodie got into her kitchen, she spread the newspaper out on the bench and turned to the article. She was hungry, deciding to get something to eat before she read it. She really shouldn't be hungry; Rupert had fed her while she was at his place. *No, not hungry, I just want something sweet.* She turned and ran upstairs to get Peg's candies.

Looking at the last of the sweets, she wondered where they had all gone and if she should get some more. She shrugged and unwrapped the candies leaving the lollipop for later. For some strange reason lollipops had never been her favorite, she would eat them if there was nothing else, but they weren't her first choice.

Once she was back in the kitchen, Jodie turned her attention to the article in front of her. It was a write up about a local guy named Lonny Richards. He had been building cubby houses since his teens. They were mostly in the wooded areas around

Wickleberry for the homeless and local kids to
play in. Not legal but no one complained, because
he did such a good job.

His parents were proud of him for making
something out of his hobby. Lonny had a brain
injury from birth. He wasn't an imbecile, but
schooling wasn't really for him. He was always
better with his hands. While still only a teenager
he helped his father with his small carpentry
business. He would take the off cuts and left-over
material from projects and use them to build
cubby houses.

Now he had been awarded a grant to continue
building, making it a true business. He would
be building cubby and tree houses for the local
community. He would build them for community
centers, childcare and designated areas for the
homeless to congregate. Jodie was thinking good
on him, he didn't let his disability stop him from
making something of himself.

She looked towards the bottom of the page,
and there was a picture of an ugly dark-haired
guy shaking the hand of their local Governor,
Sara Green. It was him! That was the guy
she had seen in her mind the other day. He
was older but it was him. He was smiling his
lopsided smile but it wasn't the crazy happy
grin she had seen. Looking at him made her

feel uncomfortable. She finished her candies and reached for the lollipop when a searing pain shot through her head.

Ψ

She was standing in a small cubby house. She could see a young girl, playing tea parties, with a boy, probably in his late teens.

'Now for dessert.' The boy said to the young girl.

She looked at him as her smile drooped and said in a small voice 'I didn't bring any.'

'That's ok.' He answered and then said 'Wanna play a special game with me instead?'

'Sure.' She answered, starting to smile again.

Jodie watched, unable to move, unable to speak, she couldn't stop what she was seeing or close her eyes. She was frozen and watched as the young girl was molested by the boy. After redressing her, he gave her a special teddy.

'This is Mr. Cubby, I made him for you, he's special and so are you.' The boy said as he gave the unsure young girl the teddy. She was confused by what just happened, but she took the hard teddy and hugged it to herself.

'We can come here for our special times together. This is our secret place for our secret game. Oh, look I forgot, I brought dessert, but I only have one, you can have it.' The boy gave the young girl a lollipop and then he took her hand and led her out of the cubby house.

Ψ

Jodie snapped back to herself. She recognized the dungarees that the young girl had been wearing. They had the initials stitched into the front pocket, J.S. It had been her! Granny Jo had stitched those initials herself after Jodie had picked out the colors of blue and lime green wool. Granny Jo had twisted the two colors together before she sewed the initials.

Jodie looked at the lollipop in her hand and threw it across the room. She angrily snatched up the newspaper and scrunched it.

Ψ

Her eyes changed to chips of ice. She stopped and opened the newspaper to the article again and looked right down at the bottom. She re-read that he would be working at Secret Forest Childcare next week. While it was closed, he would be building a cubby house for the little ones. Then further on she read that he would also be spending this weekend finishing a tree house off Gorge Grove near the old Rail Switching House. An area known for young homeless to hang out.

Ψ

Her eyes changed back. She continued to scrunch up the newspaper in her hand as she bent down and opened the cupboard then reached in and took out Mr. Cubby. She was repulsed by the feel of it. She picked the lollipop up from the floor on her way to the bin, then dumped the lot. She didn't want any of it, especially Mr. Cubby, in her home, she took her bin out to Max's trash bin. She emptied it and closed the lid. She could feel the tension leave her as she walked away.

There were enough dead already in my home. A reminder of the death of my childhood innocence shouldn't be one of them, she thought to herself as she walked back inside.

Chapter 16

The next day Max opened his bin to put his trash out, saw some that wasn't his and realized Jodie had put her trash out. But it wasn't in a trash bag. He went to throw his own in on top. He stopped and reached in as he had seen a toy. He pulled it out to take a closer look and then quickly dropped it. He knew what it was, it was a Mr. Cubby teddy, and he knew who used to make them and why. He looked towards the house over his back fence and through clenched teeth muttered 'Asshole'. He chucked his trash bag in on top and closed the lid. He turned and went back inside to get a small roll of bin bags so Jodie had something to put her trash in. It wouldn't stink for too long as rubbish was due to be collected again tomorrow morning.

Max pushed the side gate open to Jodie's place and stopped. He was surprised to see Rupert there. Max looked at himself, in his old gray cardigan and corduroy slacks and then at Rupert, who looked like he was dressed to go out to a fancy dinner. Max wondered how Harriet could ever look at him, when there was Rupert. Max walked towards Rupert smiling.

'Hey, there, what ya doin?' Max asked.

'Oh, hello. Jodie showed an interest in reading The Cove Daily. I thought I'd drop them off after I've finished reading them. Now I'm wondering where to leave this one for her. You?'

'I was just about to leave these small trash bags for her, just here on the edge of the planter by the backdoor.'

'Good then I'll leave this here too.' Rupert said as he put his newspaper down next to where Max had put the trash bags. Max picked up a big rock from the garden and put that on top to stop them from being blown away.

'It's so good having someone young in the area again.' Rupert said as he turned to leave.

'I found a Mr. Cubby toy in my trash bin, just now.' Max said. He felt like he needed to tell someone.

'Oh, really, where'd it come from?'

'I told Jodie she could put her trash in my bin…'

Rupert gasped and covered his mouth and then said through his fingers 'NO!' and he turned and looked at Jodie's place.

'Afraid so. It'd seem that summer after her parents were killed, Lonny got to her.' Max said.

'Yes, that's right, they'd just gotten that bit of money from the Inquest and Granny Jo paid Carl Richards to come around and fix the wooden siding on the house. We'd all been afraid of that possibly happening after seeing Lonny had come too.'

'Geez she'd only would've been about seven years old!'

'Do you remember what Carl did when he was confronted with the truth about what Lonny was actually doing when he "played" with the little kids? With good reason too. I know he'd hoped that burning all the Mr. Cubby's and the thrashing he gave his son would scare him enough not to do it again.'

'Carl wanted to take his son in for treatment just to be sure but Sonya wouldn't let him. She always felt guilty for Lonny almost dyin' at birth' Max continued.

'She'd no control over him being such a big baby that she couldn't birth him without assistance, I mean she almost died having him.'

'True. I guess Carl had hoped he had done enough to pull his boy into line.' Max concluded.

'That was after he'd worked here with his dad so maybe that did fix Lonny.' Rupert said hopefully.

They both looked at each other and knew in the pit of their stomachs that burning the teddys and the thrashing didn't fix anything. It only made Lonny go after those who didn't have parents to protect them or would tell on him. The homeless.

They both turned and walked towards the gate. Max went first after Rupert insisted and they turned and headed in the direction of their own homes.

Chapter 17

Jodie was wandering around inside wondering what to do today. She looked in the pantry and decided she needed to go shopping. She had the skillet; she could do pancakes if she had the mixture. That did it. She grabbed out a small tin of tuna, opened it and spooned it into her mouth as quickly as possible without wearing it. She rinsed out the can and threw it in the bin after she finished it. Then quickly ran upstairs for some money and remembered to grab her shopping bag on her way out the back door. She stopped and looked at the trash bags and paper on the edge of the planter box, scooped them up and put them inside on the bench seat in the mudroom. It made her smile, *it's so good being home*, she thought.

She locked the door behind her and walked to the shops; it was overcast today but still warm. She had money, thanks to Wendy, so she might as well have some little treats from it. She wouldn't need to sell Lillian's pills that she had nicked, perhaps she should throw them out.

****

It wasn't as busy at the shops as it had been when she came with Max to do his shopping. Jodie looked up; it looked like there might be a storm tonight. She was almost knocked over as she stopped to look up at the sky, they hadn't stopped to apologize either. *I know I'm short, but come on I'm not invisible.* Jodie shook her head and put those thoughts away.

Jodie saw a girl wearing not much more than lingerie, even though she was in public, along with huge high heels. She recognized the girl, it was Lillian. Jodie stopped and looked around, and then saw Hattie on the other side of the street wearing the skimpiest clothes that you could and still have your bits covered. It dawned on her they were hooking. She needed to keep her head down to avoid being seen. She had pinched stuff from them and even had Lillian's jeans on today.

Jodie made it into the shop without being seen. She got all sorts of things she normally wouldn't have bought but she felt like a splurge was due. As she left Lillian saw her and quickly made her way across the street towards Jodie. She didn't look happy to see Jodie. Lillian glared at her as she towered over her in the heels. So as not to make a scene Jodie let herself be led into an empty side alley.

Once around the corner, Hattie came and joined them.

'Hey, short ass, ya fuckin thief.' Lillian spat out at her.

'Hey, I still have those pills, if ya want 'em back.' Jodie said.

Hattie made a grab for Jodie's shopping bag but missed when Jodie pulled it closer to herself.

'Got enough money to be buyin' shit.' Hattie said.

'I came to get a few things for myself and a friend.' Jodie said and then regretted it.

'Oh, got yaself a Sugar Daddy, huh?' Hattie said.

'Fuck her Sugar Daddy, have you forgotten that fuckin' beating we got cause this piece of shit took those fuckin' pills! We're still out here tryin' to pay it back and fix the damage this little cunt did!' Lillian almost screamed. She pulled up her silken tank top to show Jodie the bruises on her torso. They were now a light-yellow color but they spread right across her back and up both sides.

'Yeah, I know but I'm more pissed that she took our fuckin' money. We were gonna get fuck away from this shit hole together' Hattie replied. She too pulled up her top and showed the yellowing of her bruises, they were mostly on her back.

'Look, sorry, but my head wasn't on anything but what I needed…as it is I don't know how long it's gonna last for me. You reckon you could hook me up with your guy. I might be needin' to make some cash soon.' Jodie didn't know why she said that. She had enough to deal with. She was solving her own problems, not those of others.

Lillian looked at her with suspicion but pulled a piece of card out of her bra and gave it to Jodie. *Who knew pimps had business cards these days?* 'Call this number when you're ready to join the real world' Lillian said.

Jodie took the card and as she put it in her pocket, she felt her change. She pulled it out and gave it to Lillian 'It's all I have on me. I can drop those pills back to ya.'

Lillian snatched the money and said 'Nah, call that number. Sebastian'll take care of those pills for ya.' She turned and indicated Hattie to follow and they both left the alley.

Ψ

Jodie said to herself 'Why did I do that?' Shadow whispered back *Admit it, they are out here Hooking because of you; it's now Our problem to fix.'*

Ψ

Jodie nodded to herself and walked out of the alley and back onto the sidewalk, she couldn't see Lillian or Hattie. She turned and started walking towards her home. She slowly gathered pace and then started to run. She didn't know why she was running, only that she felt the need to run and even did an extra lap around the block because she felt like she had to.

Chapter 18

Jodie let herself in the back door, picked up the roll of trash bags from the bench in the mudroom on her way through to the pantry and emptied her shopping onto the shelves. She was breathing heavily and leaned her back against the wall opposite to catch her breath. She tore off a trash bag from the roll and emptied the bin into it before putting it in the bin.

She put her shopping bag away, went over to the tap in the kitchen and turned it on. She cupped her hands and drank from them, then washed her face with the cold water. She dried her hands and face on the front of her shirt as she walked back to the mudroom. Jodie sat on the bench, unfolded the paper to read it. The bottom of the second page got her attention.

****

Missing Woman Found!

A woman reported missing by her neighbors has been found after a welfare check was paid to her residence. The Police found the back door was unsecured and gained entrance to the property. The property is on the leafy tree lined Settlers Avenue, a quiet and affluent part of Settlers Cove.

After entering the property, the Police found a distressing scene. Upon further investigation they made the grim discovery of the deceased owner.

The Police will only say that this is now an ongoing investigation.

****

Jodie smiled and decided pancakes were the ideal dinner for tonight. Time to celebrate the old bitch being dead. Jodie was feeling on edge and burnt the first couple of pancakes. She was having problems concentrating but it had nothing to do with Wendy being found. She felt like she was neglecting a duty, something she should really be doing. Stuffing her face with pancakes wasn't it. Jodie made-up half of the ready mixture and hoped that the rest would keep for tomorrow. She ate the rest of the pancakes she had already cooked then cleaned up, remembering to put the stove back in the pantry.

Chapter 19

Ψ

They came out with a hammer and some disposable gardening gloves. Just some of the extra items bought today while shopping. They smiled as they caressed the hammer they held; their eyes cold.

They collected the light jacket from the mudroom and the shopping bag out of the cupboard then put the hammer and gloves inside, looped the handles over their shoulders and wore it like a backpack. They pulled the door closed and locked it behind them.

Jodie felt like she was a co-pilot. She wasn't consciously making any of the decisions of her actions. She had a good idea where they were going. Jodie knew Shadow was in control. It should have scared her, but it didn't.

They struck out along Humphreys Street, Humphreys became Gorge Grove, once you reached the edge of the National Park. Time to find out if Lonny still had any bad habits. There was a chill in the air like it was going to rain, it was refreshing on their face.

They had just reached the sign at the start of the walking track to the old Rail Switching House when they saw a small boy walk out with a lollipop in his mouth. The boy seemed more interested in the 20 bucks in his hand than looking their way. *He doesn't pay in teddys anymore,* Jodie thought as they turned up the track and walked into the darkening shadow of the forest.

They turned a corner and then saw the monstrosity in the tree up ahead, stopped and dropped the bag off their back. They pulled out and put on the gloves and picked out the hammer. They hung the bag off the side of the bush next to them, they would collect it on the way out.

Jodie felt her heart rate go up with every step towards the treehouse and Lonny. They stopped at the bottom of the metal extension ladder; Jodie couldn't do it, she started to have doubts. She felt a creeping numbness come over her body as Shadow took full control. Then they started to move, climbing the ladder. Jodie was a passenger just along for the ride now.

They climbed to the top of the ladder and peered over the edge into the treehouse. Lonny had his back to them. When they climbed off the top of the ladder it made a noise against the edging as it moved. Lonny turned when he heard the noise.

'Hello there, little sweetie.' He said through his ugly grin, when he saw her.

They looked at him waiting for some recognition. There wasn't any. The only thing they saw in his eyes was hunger. He looked them up and down and licked his lips.

'Are you shy, now? Don't worry I won't hurt you' Lonny said in a quiet and supportive tone.

They continued to look at him. Their head tilted as Shadow tried to work out how this was going to happen. Once Shadow had a plan they took a step towards him, and he saw the hammer and laughed.

'Oh, you're here to help me build the treehouse, are you? I know of better things we can do together, just come here and I will show you how special you are.' Lonny said encouragingly to them.

They heard the word 'special' and snapped!

They screamed as they charged at him, with the hammer raised over their head ready to hit him, but he dodged them as he stepped sideways away from them. They pivoted quickly and lodged the claw of the hammer in his eye socket. He dropped dead on the spot. He hit the floor with a loud thud, shaking the platform they stood on.

The hammer caused radiating fractures extending from his eye, when it was wriggled and pried loose half of his face caved in. They peered into the hole with fascination, the hammer had punched a hole through the back of his eye into his brain. There was nothing left of his eyeball. It had exploded from the impact. They could see some pinkish goo around the edges of the hole. They looked at the hammer and laughed, there was brain goo on the hammer. They wiped it off on his clothes.

Jodie wasn't sure what was going to happen now, she felt almost cheated by how quickly it was all over. She watched with curiosity as Shadow turned their head and looked over at a roll of plastic sheeting. They dropped their hammer, dragged the roll over and laid it down beside Lonny. They went over to his tool box and rummaged around until they found his box cutter. They unrolled enough to roll Lonny up in, cut the length off. They rolled Lonny onto the plastic; it hung over his feet and head. *As tall as he was, he didn't weigh as much as Bert* Jodie thought.

They picked up their hammer, peeled back the plastic from his face. They sat on his chest. After a few good hits with the hammer, his teeth came out easily. Jodie wondered if they should just leave him lying there, then in a strange voice they said 'Nah, let him swing'.

They saw the swing arm pulley Lonny had set up to get the big items up to build the treehouse. They swung the arm in as far as it would come inside the treehouse. Lucky for them there was still one wall missing from the construction. There was enough slack in the rope to pull over to Lonny. They lifted his legs, wound one side of the pulley rope around his ankles and let them drop to the floor. They then propped up Lonny's shoulders and wrapped the rope around his neck. They let go and the rope took the tension. Lonny was hovering just over the floor. They pushed the swing arm out as hard as they could. Wanting it to get stuck in the branches of the tree on the other side of the wall. He was now out of sight, wrapped in his cocoon of plastic.

Ψ

Jodie felt herself slowly come back as she climbed down the ladder. By the time she reached the ground, she had full control of her body again. Jodie liked being in the mix of it. She had found it exhilarating being front and center while viewing and participating.

As much as she wanted to ride this high and seek out Sebastian, it was time to go home and clean up. She had some smudges of splattered gore on her but nothing hugely gross. Sebastian could wait for another day; she had pancakes to finish making and eating. She was so hungry right now.

Jodie collected her bag and put her gloves and hammer back inside and looped it over her shoulders again. As she walked out of the forest it was starting to drizzle. She shrugged and walked home.

Chapter 20

The next week Jodie divided her time between taking care of housework and hanging out with Max. Jodie always loved hearing about the history of families. Max told her how his family moved here only a handful of years after the lighthouse had been built. His family started the first local paper, The Cove Sunday Telegram and had distributed it from their home. The whole family had been involved from the collection and writing up of the stories, to creating the illustrations and later using photographs. The youngsters delivered the papers around the neighborhood.

Max had felt so grown up when he was given his first bike to help with the delivery. By that stage though, the paper had been moved over the hills and he remembered not so fondly the ride up the hills but coming down the other side had been as exhilarating as it was scary.

The paper changed its name to The Cove Daily when it moved, as it was no longer the only paper and had remained in the same building since then. Max worked his way up from delivery to running the paper. His son Max Jnr took over the paper from his father the year Granny Jo had died. The paper was still in the family.

So much history, it made her smile. She felt lighter somehow, a little bit less serious about life. She spent time talking with her parents and grandparents. They were the only ones she told, she felt that they would have approved of her claiming herself back again.

That was what it was to her. Yes, she was problem solving but she was also punishing those with false love. Not the good and real stuff but the corrosive stuff that ate away at you until you felt nothing because you were nothing to yourself anymore. You became a hollow puppet on the strings that they pulled to amuse themselves with.

Jodie felt that she had come close to becoming a puppet until they had cut her loose and now she was cutting the last of the strings. These strings still threatened to turn her into a puppet but one controlled by her past.

Chapter 21

Jodie was poking around in her rucksack; looking for something different to wear. She pulled out the now empty snacks box she had taken from Peg. She could use that in the kitchen, it would help keep her cookies fresh. Although she did like chewie cookies. *I'd find a use for it,* she thought with a shrug. She upended her bag onto her mattress and gave it a couple of extra shakes to make sure that she had gotten everything out of the corners. It was time to take stock of what she really had. The clothes she had been wearing over and over were starting to get very thin; they would soon start to fall apart. She needed to know what else she had that could replace them. Something shiny caught her attention. It was a silver lipstick case, she opened it, it was red like what Wendy used to wear. She didn't know how she had gotten it, then she saw something else that glittered in the clothes. It was some gaudy and very cheap looking jewelry. The bag with the pills was caught on the clasp of the necklace. She removed the bag and thought for a moment, she couldn't think of anything else that she needed to be doing today. *It was as good a day as any to call Sebastian.*

****

Jodie packed her bag with the pills, the lipstick and the fake jewelry. She also put in the hammer, gloves and a sharp paring knife. She wasn't sure what she would have to work with and how big or strong Sebastian was. With the others she either remembered or had a photo to go off.

Jodie walked to the public phone on the corner of Walter and Bayview Streets and called the number on the card.

'Sebastian speaking.'

'Oh, hello, a friend of mine gave me this number...' Jodie choked out.

'Spit it out, what do you want and what's your damn name?'

'I, er, took something of yours and Lillian told me to ring you to return it' Jodie rushed out.

'Oh, yeah, she said something about that, so you're the fuckin thief, what's your damn name coz she gave me none, except you're a short assed, flat chested bitch.'

'Marie my name is Marie.' Jodie didn't know why she gave him her real middle name; she should have made one up, Shadow probably would have.

'What else are ya gonna give me for the shit I had to deal with coz of your fuckin' sticky fingers?'

'Umm dunno what you're talking about.'

'Just get your ass over here and we can sort something out then. Bring my stuff to The Lookout Motel. It's at the end of Bayview Street, near the Headland Lighthouse Park. I will be in the end cabin with the "under construction" signs on the door. Ignore the signs and knock, be here within the hour!' Sebastian instructed tersely and then hung up.

Jodie hung up the receiver and walked out of the booth and headed up Bayview Street, towards the Motel.

****

Jodie stood at the end of the motel driveway, filled with doubt. What was she even doing here? Was it right?

Ψ

Shadow said, *'We're problem solving, saving ourselves is a good start, saving others is the next step.'*

Jodie nodded her head and said 'True.'

Ψ

She prepared herself mentally as she walked up the driveway, past the closed office. She could feel Shadow was with her but she was in control. They continued to the far end of the driveway for the taped off area. It was a stand-alone cabin. They saw all the signage but ignored it and knocked on the door as instructed.

A tallish junkie skinny guy answered the door. He had greasy lank black hair that hung to his collar bones. His collar bones stuck out so far that the skin was stretched tightly across them. Jodie almost laughed as she thought *so this is the fearful Sebastian that had Lillian and Hattie hooking*. Then Jodie had to remind herself that Lillian and Hattie were younger than herself by four years. The only notable feature about his face were his brown eyes; they were such a dark brown, almost ink black. He looked her up and down and then pushed the door open further, so she could squeeze in past him.

'Hi, I'm Marie' they said with the straightest face they could manage without laughing in his, as they entered.

'Geez you are a flat chested, short assed bitch ain't ya.' Sebastian said after closing the door behind them.

Shadow quickly took stock of what was in the room as Sebastian closed the door behind them. The room consisted of an old battered recliner, small table, a little kitchenette off to one side where a pile of flooring was stacked, tool boxes and other home improvement tools were stacked next to the bed. The large bed with a heavily stained mattress took up the majority of the room. Jodie didn't like him behind them, it unnerved her.

'Ok, Marie, one, where is my stuff and two, what are ya gonna give me for my troubles?'

They dropped the bag off their back and took out the small bag and handed it to him. He snatched it and started to count how many pills there were and said 'Don't worry about trying to run, I've locked the door and if you want the key, it's in my pants' he laughed as he turned and walked towards the table. While he was busy, they slipped on their gloves and took the paring knife out of their bag. He wasn't paying any attention to them.

Sebastian put his bag on the table and turned to see what she was doing. All he got to see was the small knife thrust into his eye socket. It was the last thing he ever saw out of that eye. It didn't kill him, which was why they chose to use the knife. They made sure to only maim him and not push it in too far. They wanted this dickhead to know what it felt like to be at the mercy of another.

They twisted it and ripped the knife out, his eyeball was impaled on it. Sebastian covered his eye socket with his hands and started to scream.

They dropped the knife on the floor as they punched him in the neck. His screaming irritated them. He crumpled to the floor. They weren't game to reach in and check for a pulse so they kicked him lightly, and he moaned in response. *Good he wasn't dead,* Shadow thought. They went over to the tools and found a nail gun; it didn't need a compressor for it to work. They smiled and their eyes changed to chips of ice.

Ψ

Shadow took full control and maneuvered Sebastian to the floor at the bottom of the bed. She splayed out his arms in a mock pose of the crucifixion that hung on the wall behind the bedhead and nailed his right hand to the floor. He tried to scream but couldn't as his larynx was too swollen from their punch earlier. He tried pulling his hand back up off the floor with the other one. Shadow stood on his arm and forced that hand down and nailed it to the floor as well.

Sebastian tried to say something. Through his swollen neck he sounded like he was barking. Shadow guessed from his eye movements it was for her to take the cash and drugs that were sitting on the table if she would just leave. It made her laugh. She went to pull down one of his legs and he kicked out at her, she jumped back then kicked him hard in the ribs. He coughed out a strangled cry and was too distracted by the blinding pain in his ribs to worry about what she was doing with his legs. He tried to kick her again after she nailed the first leg to the floor through his ankle. She stood up, calmly walked up and looked down at him. He was such a pitiful sight, with tears streaming down his face. Shadow squatted down to get a better look. One side of his face was stained by the bloody tears from his ruined eye socket. She stood and turned then stomped on his groin, he grunted and tried to curl up in pain. She pulled the other leg down and nailed that to the floor. She put the nail gun down as she reached for and unzipped his jeans. She reached in and felt around but the key was in his jocks. *Sick bastard* Shadow thought as she removed the key, and didn't bother to tuck anything in before she forcefully zipped his jeans back up.

She watched as his body spasmed in pain. *How could he feel that over the rest of the pain assaulting his body?* Shadow thought as she picked up the nail gun, leaned over him and put one more nail into him, through his neck. He didn't die straight away. Shadow was fascinated by the red bubbles coming out from around the nail. She watched them bubble up around the nail head as he tried to breathe. She sat down and leaned in close to hear them make their little popping noises. She got a bit too close, and felt the warm blood splatter lightly on her cheek when they popped. She got up, leaving the nail gun on the floor as she wandered over to where the knife was dropped. She tried to flick his deflated eyeball off the blade, but the mess wouldn't move, which made her laugh. She wiped it off on the end of the mattress then put it in their bag and got out the hammer. She could have used his as there was one sitting on the kitchenette bench, but it didn't feel like the right thing to do. She stood over him looking down into his pleading black eye. Shadow held eye contact and smirked as she stepped across his chest and straddled his body. She kept eye contact as she bashed in the front of his face. She pulled the teeth she wanted out, and put them in her pocket. She put the hammer away and got the lipstick and jewelry out and threw them on the bed. They didn't belong to Jodie and Shadow had no use for them so he may as well have them.

Shadow put the bag over her shoulder, unlocked the door, threw the key into the room and closed the door behind her. She sauntered down the driveway, along the sidewalk and dumped their gloves in separate trash bins as they headed home. She knew the bins would be emptied first thing in the morning.

Ψ

Chapter 22

Jodie woke the next morning remembering what they did last night. It was better being there, but she still had gaps in her memory. She could remember stabbing him in the eye. She then saw the nail gun and after that it was flashes of pictures until they were walking back up the road coming home. Some of last night was still hidden from her.

She remembered seeing the fake jewelry and lipstick on the mattress. She had in the back of her mind that if he had told anyone 'Marie' was coming around the fake jewelry and lipstick could be taken as hers. Jodie heard Shadow laugh in the back of her mind, that made her smile as she stretched. Then she wondered what she would do today, her stomach rumbled.

After getting dressed, with the idea of visiting the neighbors after breakfast, she had pancakes still to make. Jodie headed downstairs and kissed her hand and then placed it on the door to the basement and

134

said, 'Love you all' as she walked past the door. It had become a morning and night ritual when she passed the door to the basement. She almost skipped into the kitchen, she felt so light and happy.

Jodie noticed something yellow on the floor that had been shoved under the back door. It was an envelope. Instead of turning into the pantry, Jodie walked over and picked up the envelope. She opened it and pulled out a delightfully colorful card. It was addressed to her;

Jodie,
I am requesting your attendance at a women's day at my place. There will be sandwiches, soda and good music. Hope you can join us.
Harriet

Jodie looked at it and wondered when it was to start as there wasn't any time on it, not that she had a clock anyway. A "Woman's Day" meant that there would be other females there and the only other woman around here was Margery. Could be fun. Jodie put the pretty card back in the envelope and put it on the kitchen bench. Jodie sniffed herself. She didn't stink and she looked clean and tidy, then she remembered a cute black top that she had found yesterday.

She ran back upstairs. She had separated and neatly folded her clothes into piles yesterday and placed them in a line along the back wall of her room. She walked over and squatted down next to the pile of tops, she noticed something crusty on her jeans, it was probably from last night. Jodie remembered she still had that nice set of clothes she was given for a court appearance. She changed into the light blue lace edged top and pale gray linen pants. She stood looking down at herself, it was the best that she could do.

Chapter 23

It was a warm day out of the house. Before leaving she had wondered if she should have brought a jacket with her. She enjoyed the warm sun on her face and arms. There was a bounce in her step as she crossed the street and walked up to Harriet's place. Jodie lightly knocked on the front door, she suddenly felt awkward and shy. The door opened so quickly, Jodie didn't have time to turn and run.

'Oh, there you are, we weren't sure if you were coming' Margery said with a smile as she answered the door, she turned and said over her shoulder 'Harry, Jodie's here.'

'Good, good, don't leave her standing on the front step, let her in!' Jodie heard.

Margery stepped back allowing Jodie's entrance. Jodie hadn't met Margery before. She had been spending her time mostly with Max and Rupert. Although she had visited Syd, he made her skin crawl and she didn't want Shadow hurting him so she hadn't gone back even though she was invited.

She tried not to stare. Max had told her that Margery was in her 50s but not what she looked like. Margery had bleached blonde hair and dark red lipstick. She looked like an aged pin up girl from the 1950's. Her figure was probably a bit fuller than it used to be, but she still dressed well. This made Jodie a little bit uncomfortable in her own clothes.

They walked down the hallway to the kitchen area. There was a large round table in the middle of the room and Harriet was standing next to it making a drink. Harriet turned and passed the drink to Jodie.

'Thank you.' Jodie said as she took it.

Harriet was everything Margery wasn't, her hair was a natural looking chestnut brown. She was slender, athletic, in a white t-shirt, blue jeans and no makeup. She didn't look like she was in her 70's!

'Now we can start this woman's day, we're all here.' Harriet said.

'Thank you for inviting me, Harriet...' Jodie began.

'Oh, no, no my dear, I am Harry, and this is Margie, or would you like for me to call you Jodie Marie?' Harry said with a smile to take this sting out of her comment.

'Ok, thanks for the invite, Harry. Not sure....' Jodie stammered.

'It's alright, dear, I just thought that instead of just Margie and I getting together that we should have you here as well. It's so good that you are back in the old neighborhood again. So good to have you home, you look delightful, the blue of that top brings out the color of your eyes. Please sit, I'll put on some music and then we can talk and eat. Yes, please eat.' Harry said as she pulled out a chair for Jodie and then pointed to the piles of sandwiches and smiled at her.

Jodie smiled shyly back and then sat down but she stood up again and took the plate Margie gave her. Jodie put only a couple of sandwiches on it.

'Here, take some more, lord knows I shouldn't be eating so many of them myself' Margie said as she stacked about half dozen more of the small, neatly cut triangles on Jodie's plate.

That made Jodie smile, she sat down with her plate and put it on the table, she had a sip of the soda and liked the sound that the ice cubes made as they moved around in the glass, tinkling together.

Ψ

'Nothing like delightful little bubbles of blood popping' Shadow whispered in the back of Jodie's mind.

Ψ

This beats something out of a can any day Jodie thought. Just then some sort of music came on, it wasn't modern, more like what Granny Jo used to listen to. It made Jodie want to dance; she shuffled around in her seat.

Harry came back dancing to the music, she saw Jodie and pulled her up from her seat and they danced together. Jodie pulled Margie up and they all were laughing and dancing. Margie was the first back to the table for something to eat. Jodie ran her hand over her head. Her hair was starting to get long. She wondered if Harry had any clippers.

Harry saw her run her hand over her head and said, 'Jo always preferred short hair too.' It took Jodie a fraction of a second to realize that Harry had been speaking of her Granny Jo.

'Jo pretty much had the same haircut from the first time I met her to the day she passed. I only ever saw her hair reach her shoulders twice in the time I knew her. We were friends and neighbors for close to 40 years. She said that she didn't like the feeling of her hair on her shoulders. I believed it was really because once her hair got past her ears it started to curl and she didn't like the curls' Harry explained.

'I prefer mine short too, do you know if anyone has any clippers?' Jodie asked.

'Oh, I have a set!' Margie said, she stood up and disappeared down the hallway, Jodie heard the front door as it opened and then closed.

Harry smiled 'Now, you are in for it' she laughed and then added as she saw Jodie's frightened face 'Don't worry Margie used to be a makeup and hair stylist. She keeps me looking so good, you wouldn't even know that I am pure white under this color!'

'Oh, wow, I'd thought that was your own color!' Jodie replied.

'Oh, no dear I haven't been my own color for decades, eat up she'll be back soon enough.'

No sooner than Harry said this they heard the front door open and close again. Margie came back in with her "kit".

It became a real woman's day after that. There was laughing, eating, talking and hair styling. Well, Jodie's had been shaved; Margie shaved a few patterns into it before taking it all off to a number one. Harry wasn't sure about it being that short, but Margie had pointed out how thick Jodie's hair was. Even with it being that short it was hard to see her scalp. Harry had curls put into her own hair. Then Margie had taken out her makeup and did Harry's face. She looked like she was in her 40's by the end, Margie was truly talented. Jodie had her own makeup done, she had tried to stop Margie, but she was talked into it by Harry.

When Jodie looked in the mirror afterwards, she had been stunned that she could look like that. The only time she had makeup on before was when the girls had been "done up" by Martha. Harry brought out a camera and Margie took photos of Harry and Jodie. Jodie wasn't comfortable but Margie soon had her laughing and posing.

It was probably the most fun Jodie had ever had with other people since her Granny Jo had passed. Jodie was almost sad when the day started to get dark and it was time to go home.

She promised that she would come again the next time there was a woman's day. She left with a paper plate full of small sandwiches.

Chapter 24

Jodie decided to visit Max on her way home. She had planned to visit him today anyway; she just hoped it wasn't too late to be visiting. She walked in his back gate and knocked on the back door. She was thinking of leaving when the door opened. Max looked distracted.

'Are you alright?' Jodie asked.

'I'm fine, here, come in, we need to talk' Max said as he ushered her inside. Once inside and the door closed, Jodie followed Max through his place. Max had converted the small study area into a bedroom years ago when getting up the stairs had become harder. The only time he went up now was to have a bath then he used the chairlift to get there. Truthfully once he was living by himself, he felt more secure and cozier down in the study than in one of the larger rooms upstairs.

He indicated for her to sit in the big lounge chair and he sat on his bed. He didn't have any furniture in his living room anymore, he had given it away years ago. His son didn't have any interest in visiting his dad, he hated the old neighborhood. Max Jnr lived in Settlers Cove with his family. The grand and great grandchildren never visited Wickleberry if they could help it. It was sad. Families aren't meant to be like that.

'Jodie, there were a couple o' cops here lookin' for you today' he waited for her to nod and then he continued 'Your Great Aunt Wendy died and her Will stated that you're to inherit everythin'. The problem is that they've also been to your ol' Group Home. We're to keep an eye out for you and to get you to go in and see the cops.' Max said slowly.

Max waited for a response; he wasn't upset that the old bitch was dead, but he wondered if Jodie would be. When it didn't seem that she was going to respond Max continued 'I know some o' the shit you had to deal with when you lived with her' Max was now watching Jodie as she continued to stare at the floor. 'Also, the little bit you've told me about what happened over at the Group Home and what they'd wanted of you... you can stay here with me, until you decide what you're going to do.' Max finished.

'Oh, ok, no, no, why can't they just leave me the fuck alone? Look Max thanks for the offer, but I can't. It's good I guess that the old bitch is dead but... I dunno, it would be nice to have nice stuff, I guess but, it's not the things I grew up with!' Jodie finished in a rush.

'I hear you; you want what that old hag sold off; the family stuff, not her shit. I didn't tell them where to find you 'cause I wasn't sure if you wanted that. While you make up your mind Jodie, try to remember everything that went to Wendy, the money, the house and shares all came from your Great Granddad, Granny Jo's dad Norman Fielder, remember that.'

'True, just leave it with me and I'll let you know what I decide to do, ok? Here you take these sandwiches, I'm not hungry.'

'Sure.'

Jodie left Max's place feeling bewildered about the fact that Wendy had left everything to her. Her head kept turning it over inside her mind. What should she do, the money would be nice but the house, nope! She stopped herself from thinking of that place. *It had been hell on Earth for me and we'd killed Wendy there.*

Chapter 25

It had been a lovely and unexpected day but now reality had come crashing back in. As Jodie got ready for bed, everything, every hurt feeling, every horrible experience and everything she had learnt to do to survive, was jumping around inside of her brain demanding attention. She knew she wouldn't be able to sleep, instead she walked down to the basement to talk it all through with her family. She needed to verbalize it and not just let it bounce around inside of her head. She hoped it would help.

Jodie sat on the bottom step, she hadn't bothered to turn on any of the lights, she found the darkness tonight comforting. She felt hidden and safe, there was a small amount of light coming in through the easement windows. It made the dark less black. Behind her on the stairs a black shadow formed as Jodie spoke and told her family everything.

Martha and Jon had a nice little set up, they took the really abused and traumatized children, the ones that had been bounced from every other Group or Foster Home. This gave them a good standing in the community because they had to deal with the worst cases. It also meant that no one believed anything that the children said about Martha and Jon Samson and how their Group Home was really run.

Martha and Jon would let the newly arrived have two days to themselves and then they would be introduced to how things really were. If they wanted more blankets, pillows other than the two they were given when they first arrived or breakfast and dinner and not just lunch every day, they had to earn it. That was when they were sized up and were grouped. Each group catered to a different clientele, like Ethnic girl/boy or sweet girl/masculine boy. They never got paid but it made their stay at the Group Home "easier". There was never any intercourse but there was plenty of touching, fingering, oral and kissing.

Jodie knew that by taking Sebastian down there would be repercussions. He had worked for Martha and Jon; Sebastian hadn't done anything with the children from their Group Home that they hadn't already approved of. Sebastian arranged the clientele that 'visited' the children three nights a week. Jodie knew all of this from being there.

They had a good and steady stream of clients that came to town to have their perverted thirsts quenched. Some of them were famous or held high positions in the community from legal to government. They knew how to keep their heads down and helped keep Martha and Jon's empire out of the spotlight and safe. They made sure that Martha and Jon were awarded the biggest slice of the funding pie.

If you proved a good "earner" and loyal then you would be given other tasks, like selling pills or shoplifting. If you were willing to do either of those, you got to keep some of the "profits". However, if you disappointed them then you would be handed over to Sebastian "to be sorted out" and made to work off what you "owed". This is what had happened to Lillian and Hattie, when Jodie had taken those pills. They hadn't just been for Lillian to sell but Hattie as well. Hattie was a good shoplifter and pickpocket, a good earner for them. Jodie remembered the bruising and it just proved it didn't matter how good you were at earning for them, if you stepped out of line then you were punished. It didn't matter that Lillian and Hattie were only teenagers, Sebastian happily put them out on the streets, hoping to earn the money back for the pills.

Martha and Jon were in charge, Sebastian helped to maintain discipline and kept things running smoothly. If anyone proved to be beyond their control but might still be of use to them in the future, they were railroaded into the prison system. Those who were totally uncontrollable were handed over to the Monroe brothers, Tony and Neil. They helped to make the disobedient disappear. Jodie wasn't entirely sure how they did that but she guessed they killed the problematic person as they weren't ever seen again. She knew she had come very close to this happening to her when she had sliced up her client. She got lucky when they kicked her out of the system. She might not have held any value to them back then and until now she probably hadn't even entered their minds. That had changed, Martha and Jon knew she was worth a staggering amount of money, her worth had skyrocketed and that put a very large target on her back.

She didn't want to stay with Max; it would put him in harm's way. Jodie was wondering why she hadn't just dealt with her own issues and why she had decided to try and "help" Lillian and Hattie, when the system still had such a tight grip on them. Sebastian didn't have to die.

Ψ

She heard Shadow behind her on the stairs laughing, then say, *'You enjoyed it.'*

Jodie half-turned and saw the dark shape of Shadow sitting behind her. Jodie felt her blood run cold and she shivered but she didn't move, instead she turned fully and spoke to Shadow.

'No, it was you who enjoyed it!' Jodie yelled.

Shadow laughed and said *'But what am I? I'm just a part of you, the part you have kept buried, hidden and tried to forget existed. I'm every hurt feeling, every persecution you have endured, every wrong deed done to you by others to amuse themselves. I'm also your strength, perseverance, preservation and the only part of you that can remember it all! Without me you would have been dead long ago either by your own hand or those of others.'*

'But you tricked me into believing I was fixing problems, not creating them! Now it has all followed me back here, to the only place I have ever belonged with the only people who ever loved me!' Jodie screamed.

'Hush. I guess we have some more work to do yet. Think about it. Bert and Dorothy had finished working in the system, exposing their misdeeds needed to be done. Martha and Jon are comfortable,

well set up and protected. Getting to them won't be easy but we have already started to trim their reach, by getting rid of Sebastian. Think about it, how much more damage to their empire we can do if we get rid of Tony and Neil!' Shadow explained.

'Problem solving....' Jodie mumbled to herself.

'Problem solvers.' It was the last thing Jodie heard as the dark form hugged her and then faded as it flowed into her. Jodie got up as if sleep walking and climbed the stairs. She closed the basement door behind her before turning and slowly walking towards the stairs up to her own room.

Ψ

Chapter 26

The next day was bright and clear and Jodie woke feeling rested and at peace with herself. She stretched and got up, stopped at the bathroom before heading down to the kitchen. She walked to the back door and opened it; some fresh air would be nice. If they were going to come for her, they wouldn't be coming in the daytime. No one could really look in with the six-foot fence around the backyard anyway. Jodie looked around for something to hold the door open so it wouldn't slam closed. She looked outside and saw a good-sized rock in the planter box, it was holding down a newspaper. It must have been from Rupert, she picked up the rock and paper then wedged the backdoor open. She was going to make something to eat but decided to get the stove out and make herself a nice cup of tea instead.

As the water boiled on the stove, she put the tea bag in it. Jodie didn't have any cups; she would just drink it out of the saucepan. She opened the paper and read it. She saw that there was a small shopping strip approved for development, just this side of the hills. It was probably to cater to the suburban spread from Settlers Cove. She had noticed all the new construction of houses being built on some of the smaller hills this side. However, it would make it more convenient than walking the distance she did now to the older and larger one. It was about a three-mile round trip from here. Wendy's place was closer. Jodie wondered once she had finished with their "problem solving", if she could somehow "buy" this place back. She didn't know who owned it, but she would be in a better position to find out once she had money.

There were a couple of articles in the paper that got her attention. The saucepan began boiling. She turned off the stove. She put a few soup spoons of sugar into the saucepan and stirred them until they dissolved. Then she picked up the saucepan by the handle and went over to the tap and turned it on. She always let it run for a little bit, there was still some rusty water coming out. It was from the old pipes, they probably needed to be replaced. She let some of the clean water run into the saucepan and then turned off the tap. She stirred her tea in the saucepan again and carefully took a sip from the lip. It was still a little bit warm, so she decided to let it sit and cool as she read the paper. She put it back down on the stove and turned her attention to the first of the articles that had caught her eye.

****

Grisly Murder at The Lookout Motel

The owner was found dead early this morning by a long-term resident. After Sebastian Nelson failed to open the front office, the resident went to his cabin to find him. When he had no response to his knocking, he found the door was unlocked. He entered and discovered the grisly scene of the murdered Mr. Nelson.

Police are unwilling to go into details of the injuries that were inflicted upon the victim. They are now calling this an ongoing investigation.

****

Jodie smiled; he was found quicker than she had thought but he was dead when he was found.

Jodie turned her attention to the other article on the opposite page.

****

Missing Couple

Bert and Dorothy Smythe, recent recipients of "Service to the Community Award" for their years of service, devotion and of caring for Foster Children have been reported missing.

A friend of the couple had a prearranged meeting with Mrs. Smythe. She was to collect a few bunches of dried herbs for her cooking. When she went to get them, there wasn't an answer at the door. She knocked for several minutes but it went unanswered. She had a look around and their van was still in the shed, nothing seemed missing. She noticed unusual digging in the herb garden and called the Police.

The Police will not comment on what was found at the scene. They would very much like to talk to Mr. and Mrs. Smythe regarding what was discovered. The police are asking the public for their assistance in locating the missing couple.

****

They had found those children, good. Jodie laughed as they hadn't found Bert and Dorothy yet. Jodie guessed they would eventually realize what was in the new steps around the side. Shadow must have done a good job sealing it. The smell hadn't leaked!

So far it was looking to be a good day. Then Jodie turned to the last page and it got better.

******

Missing Man
Mr. Lonny Richards was reported missing by his father Carl this morning. Lonny had been working on building a treehouse for the homeless over

the weekend. Carl knew that Lonny had planned on sleeping there to finish the project. He hadn't expected his son back until Monday morning. When he didn't show and couldn't be reached on his cell phone, Carl went to look for him but was unable to locate his son.

The Police are now handling this as a missing person case.

****

Jodie knew they hadn't hidden Lonny that well. Carl either found him and didn't want to deal with it or hadn't bothered to go looking. Still, that was another problem solved.

Jodie spent most of the day wandering around the house and fenced yard, envisaging how it could look after she bought it back. She was going to go in next week and present herself so she could collect the family money. It had never been Wendy's; it came from Granny Jo's dad's family. Even though Wendy was Norman's daughter too, she never understood the meaning of family. It was still odd that she had left everything to Jodie. Jodie knew it had nothing to do with the idea of family, probably more to do with keeping it away from everyone else.

Chapter 27

Jodie was getting ready to go have dinner with Max as they had already agreed. Every second Friday night she would have dinner with him. He liked to feel as though he was looking after her. Jodie knew it was a little bit of that, but also so he didn't feel lonely. She pulled on a white t-shirt and it ripped, she needed to find something else to wear. She had enough cash to buy more clothes, she should have done that today, instead of wandering around letting her imagination take control. It didn't really matter; she could go tomorrow. She found a black t-shirt with little silver stars on the sleeves and put that on instead. Jodie was running late, she hurried down the stairs and out the backdoor. She pulled it closed and locked it behind her, she was about to go through the gate when she heard a smashing noise from Max's house. She froze and listened. Then she heard a noise like someone was trying to yell but was being smothered.

Ψ

Jodie started to pant and then her eyes changed. Shadow took a deep breath and slowly let it out. She turned, went back and unlocked the backdoor. She collected the hammer and a small sharp paring knife. She walked back out the back door, quietly closed it, but didn't bother to lock it. She didn't go through the gate; she climbed the old Weeping Willow in the backyard, and dropped down into Max's backyard.

She landed lightly on her feet at the back of his vegie patch in the soft soil. She carefully made her way to the back of the house and peered in the kitchen window. She saw nothing from that angle. She moved to the side of the house and looked into the lounge room window. She saw Tony Monroe standing on Max's hand as he lay prone on the floor. Neil was standing in the doorway to the kitchen keeping a lookout. Tony was twisting the toe of his shoe on Max's hand breaking his bones. Max covered his mouth with his other hand to try and stifle his screams of pain. *Bless him he's trying to keep Jodie safe, but without me she wouldn't still be here,* Shadow thought.

She knew she needed to separate the brothers as she wouldn't be able to take them together. She would have to be quick and deadly; she steeled herself for what she must do. She went back around to the backdoor and tapped gently.

She hoped only one came to the door, if it was Neil all the better, he was only a handful of inches taller than herself. She was ready, hammer in one hand and the knife in the other. She heard someone walking heavily towards the door, the old floorboards squeaked as they stomped their way towards her.

The door was yanked open. It was Neil. That was all that registered before she struck. She thrust the small knife into his eye as hard as she could. The blade went in so far that her fingers went into his eye socket as well. Neil was dead before he started to collapse, she pulled him towards her, so he fell out the door and not with a thump on the floorboards. She didn't bother to retrieve the knife; she stepped over and around him as she went inside. She looked at getting another knife when she heard…

'Neil, who's at the door, Neil, what the hell…old man, who are you expecting? Tell me!' It was Tony.

She had to move quickly, before he did any more damage to Max. She could hear Max making choking noises then a slight scream escaped him. That last noise unstuck her and she moved towards the living room. She picked up the cutting board as she walked past it. Wrapping her fingers around the handle, feeling the hardness of the wood. Three more steps and she was at the threshold to the lounge room. Tony was kneeling pressing his knee into Max's throat. He was also bending each of Max's fingers back. She heard the crunch as they splintered or popped out of joint. He was so intent on torturing Max that he wasn't aware she was there. She threw the hammer; it collected Tony in the side of his head and knocked him off Max. Tony was only stunned a short while and soon started to get back up. Which was enough of a pause for her. She ran screaming at him with the chopping board in both hands. She mowed him down; she collected him full in the face with the board. His head snapped back from the force and the momentum knocked him over. His head landed heavily on the hearth extension tiles. Before he could move, she held the board in one hand as she swung it down, bludgeoning him with it. When it splintered from the force, she picked up the hammer and continued with that. She only stopped when her hammer cracked his skull open and she was splattered with his brains. She blinked as she wiped his brains off her face and her eyes changed back.

Ψ

Max lay horrified on the floor, trying to breathe. He was scared shitless by what he had just witnessed. Jodie looked at him and then moved towards him and knelt beside him. He couldn't help it; he flinched away from her.

Max watched her look at him, hurt by his reaction to her, she looked around confused. She shook her head, didn't say a word. She stood up slowly, she didn't bother to try and help him up. Her head was still bowed and then she looked at him again and her eyes were like chips of ice and she smiled, it almost scared him to death. He was relieved when she turned and walked out of the room.

As Max laid on the floor and took stock of his injuries, three fingers on his right hand were either broken or dislocated. His little finger was the worst, blood oozed out where the bone had ruptured through the skin. He was having problems breathing, and he gently felt his throat with his left hand which was mostly undamaged. His throat was probably just bruised from the bastard's knee. Max continued his injury assessment, lightly feeling his ribs, every breath brought him a blinding, stabbing pain from probably a few broken ribs. Max remembered that the shorter of the two assholes had stomped on him.

Having finished his assessment of his injuries he carefully rolled over and belly crawled along the floor, using his legs and left hand to push and

Luise Cowen

pull him towards the kitchen. He got there to see the feet of the other guy disappear out of his open back door. He couldn't see Jodie anywhere. When her eyes changed color, it scared him to the very heart of his being, and her smile was just pure evil. Max propped himself up against the doorway into the kitchen, it hurt more sitting up. He stayed sitting as he felt less exposed with his back against something. He looked around and knew he would have to call the Police to try and explain what had happened. He sat there trying to think of a plausible story to explain all the carnage. From where he was, he could see blood, flesh and bone, splattered up the brick chimney; some had even reached the ceiling. He had ten-foot ceilings!

He saw the chopping board; it was made of a single piece of Ironwood and now it was splintered into two pieces. It was a wedding gift when he had gotten married all those years ago. He turned his attention back to the dead guy, laying in a pool of gore on his floor. He didn't have a face anymore, hell, he didn't have a head!

Max heard a noise behind him, he carefully turned his head, his neck hurt, and looked. It was Jodie. She looked at him and he could see the concern on her face and the normal blue of her eyes.

'I took care of the other one. The Weeping Willow needed fertilizing anyway. Can't tell where

162

he had fallen. Now it looks like just the one guy was here' Jodie said in a flat lifeless voice.

As much as she had scared him earlier, he wanted to hug her and reached for her. She crumpled, landed heavily on her knees next to him. She hugged him gently and he hugged her with as much strength as he could, it hurt but it was worth it. He wasn't sure what had just happened, but he knew that she was the only reason he was still alive. He pushed her away and looked at her. He was surprised to see that she wasn't crying as he was.

'Get my cell phone, please, it's just on the chair in my room' Max said.

Jodie got up and went and got it. She returned and gave it to him as she said 'I guess you have to call the Police now.'

He looked at her and nodded and then said 'I'll say I did it, that I killed him in self-defense' he looked over at what was left of the guy 'I'll say I was fighting for my life, that way it'll explain all the damage to him. They should believe that...' As he talked Jodie moved over to what was left of Tony and stuck her fingers into the mess that used to be his face, pulled out some teeth and put them in her pocket. It made Max want to vomit, but Jodie was still looking at him while she did it. He didn't think she had even been aware of what she had been doing.

Ψ

When she put them in her pocket, she said in a strange little voice that sent chills down his spine 'another set, good, both done now.'

Ψ

'You better get home, Jodie' Max told her.
    'No.'
    'Don't argue with me, let me do this, now go!'

Ψ

Jodie heard Shadow say *'Listen to him we don't need to be here.'*

Ψ

Max saw Jodie's face go slack and she nodded, got up and walked out of the room like she was in a daze. Max waited until he heard the side gate rattle as it closed. That was when he started to dial for the Police and Ambulance.

Chapter 28

Jodie woke to the morning light seeping in through one of the easement windows. She was laying on the basement floor on her mattress with all her personal stuff scattered around her. She kept getting flashes in her head of last night. She knew why she was down here; she was hiding out. She should have really left and gone somewhere else but there wasn't anywhere else for her to go. It was better for her to be here with her family anyway.

She had been vaguely aware of the sirens and noise last night as the Ambulance and Police cars arrived at Max's. She wanted to go and see him at the Hospital, but she had to wait until someone told her what had happened. She knew no one would come by to tell her while there were Police around, she was squatting after all.

She had some idea how Neil and Tony had found Max but it had happened so quickly. Wendy's home address would have been in her file that Martha and Jon had, as she was her next of kin. However, everyone on this side of the hills knew that this was her old neighborhood. It would not take much to work out that this was her old home and Max was an old family friend.

She suddenly felt so stupid when she saw a flash of her burying Neil under the Weeping Willow. She should have taken him somewhere else; anywhere else. He never lived here, he had no right to be buried here. This was her family's home, only her family deserved to be resting here. She suddenly felt like she had contaminated the sanctity of her family's home.

After a few more hours of beating herself up mentally with what she should and should not have done, Jodie laughed when she felt herself start to jiggle around on her butt, she needed to pee badly. She bum scooted to the end of the mattress and stood up. She stretched as she walked to the stairs and wondered if it was safe to go up. Her bladder reminded her how full it was; with a shrug she climbed the stairs. She was careful, she opened the door and listened intently for any noise before she moved. She made her way to the downstairs toilet and peed into the stagnant water; she knew she wouldn't have made it upstairs. She could feel crusty stuff caught in her eyelashes. Not sure if it were hers or from last night, she decided to wash her face in the kitchen sink. Jodie checked and saw that the backdoor was closed and locked. She went to the sink and turned on the tap, the water ran clear enough for her to roughly scrub her face with her hands. The cold water was refreshing. She walked into the pantry, pulled the trash bag out of the bin and left it on the bottom shelf. She then emptied all the shelves into the bin. The gas cylinders were the last in and she carefully balanced them on top. She picked up the stove and carried that in her other hand. She might have been overreacting, no one had come charging into her place. Jodie made her way across the dining room and peeked out of the corner of the window from behind the curtain. She couldn't see anything moving outside. She gave a sigh of relief, then she saw a Police Patrol car slowly cruise past her place. She turned and ran back down to the basement.

Jodie sat on her mattress making groupings of her food. She looked at the empty trash can and shrugged, she would be using that as a toilet. It was too risky going upstairs any time soon.

Chapter 29

It was almost a full week before anyone came to tell Jodie what had happened to Max. She was in the kitchen, drinking from the tap. The water out of the basement taps always ran rusty and she needed to get a drink. She heard a light tapping on the backdoor. She froze, not sure what to do. Then the tapping stopped and the rhythm of one of Granny Jo's favorite songs was being tapped on the backdoor. Jodie knew then it was Harry. Jodie was careful as she walked towards the backdoor and peeked out the side of the curtain. All she could see was Harry, good she was alone.

Jodie opened the door just enough for Harry to come inside and then closed it quickly and quietly behind her. Harry couldn't contain herself and as soon as Jodie had turned back to face her, she grabbed hold of Jodie in a fierce but caring hug.

'So good to see you. I've terrible news. I couldn't come until all the cops had left. They're still doing rounds, mostly at night now.' Harry said into Jodie's ear as she held her in the hug.

She pushed Jodie away and continued 'Some guy broke into Max's place and attacked him. Max is still Hospital, thankfully the cops aren't going to charge him with anything. It was self-defense; Max was fighting for his life and he made a bit of a mess of the guy apparently' Harry pulled Jodie back into another hug.

'Oh no' It was all Jodie could think to say.

'It'll be alright. Max is in good spirits; I've been spending as much time as I can with him while he's in Hospital. He should be home again next week. Although his bastard son believes that Max shouldn't be living alone at his age and now is eyeing off selling the house to force Max into a nursing home!' Harry went on.

'No, that isn't right' Jodie said.

'I know, right, but all of us here will show them all that we have our own little community here. We take care of one another.' Harry explained.

She has no idea how true that is Jodie thought.

Harry pushed Jodie away, finally breaking the long hug. She reached into the satchel bag hanging off her shoulder and pulled out some newspapers. Jodie looked at them, confused.

'Rupert said he had been giving you his old newspapers to read. He saved them all from this past week. When I said that I was going to come over and fill you in on what had been happening around here, he told me to give them to you' Harry said with a funny half smile.

'Oh, thank you and to him,' Jodie said, not knowing what else to say.

'Ok, I better get going. I have some errands to do before I go back to the Hospital and visit Max again. I'll let him know I've seen you and have filled you in' Harry said and then she turned and opened the backdoor. She only opened it enough for her to slip out and then she closed it again behind herself.

Jodie couldn't help but smile. Max had finally got Harry's attention. Jodie locked the back door, put the newspapers under her arm and turned and walked back down to the basement. She still felt exposed up here in the house.

Chapter 30

There had been some good reading in those newspapers and some disturbing articles too.

-They had located Lonny Richards; his body had been found.

-Martha and Jon were under investigation for their mistreatment of juveniles at their Group Home.

-The missing couple, Bert and Dorothy had been located, they were deceased.

-Then there was a large write up by one of the paper's journalists about the possibility of a serial killer with so many people now having been killed in the areas of Settlers Cove and Wickleberry.

-Then there was another article about the attack on Max Branley and his ongoing recovery.

Jodie reread the newspapers front to back several times but couldn't find anything to support the journalist's article. *They were just shaking the tree to see what, if anything, fell out.* They even had a tip line number at the bottom of the article.

It made Jodie smile; she didn't think that the Police would have been happy when they saw that.

There was something else too in the back of Jodie's mind. If a journalist was able to link up the murders, then the Police probably had as well.

****

Jodie rummaged around in her bag until she found the envelope from Harry. It took a bit longer, but she found a pencil that she could write with. She felt she needed to do this. She felt like she was struggling for control of her body. Shadow was screaming in the back of Jodie's mind *'DON'T DO THIS, THERE IS NO NEED TO DO THIS!!!'* repeatedly.

Jodie fought for and gained control of herself and wrote out her own Will, on the back of the invitation. It wasn't because she was going to kill herself, but to make sure the family money didn't go to the state!

She left everything to Max Branley and Harriet Grant. She knew that they would know what to do with it, to help everyone who mattered.

Jodie just managed to finish writing Max and Harriet's names on the front of the envelope when a searing hot pain ripped through Jodie's brain and she passed out.

Chapter 31

Jodie had no idea how long she had lain there half on her mattress and half on the cold concrete floor. She was cold and stiff. She was trying to concentrate on what had woken her; it was a male voice and now she could feel herself being lifted.

'Got a good strong pulse, she's alive. Careful now, make sure you get her in the center of the stretcher.'

Jodie tried to open her eyes, they felt like they had been glued shut. She eventually got one eye open. Everything was blurry, she couldn't focus and the bouncing started to make her feel sick, so she closed it again.

Nothing was making much sense; she felt the warmth of the sun on her face and then it was gone. She felt the stretcher dip, she guessed that she was inside a vehicle. Someone did some straps up across her body, then she heard the doors slam shut, before it started to move.

****

Jodie woke up in Hospital, she looked around the room. She had it to herself. She was restrained with padded cuffs at her ankles and wrists to the bed. There was a drip in her arm. A Policewoman sat in a chair by the door.

Jodie tried to sit up, the movement caught the Policewoman's attention, she looked up. She stood up and opened the door, leaned out and spoke softly to someone else just outside and then closed the door and sat back down again. She did not acknowledge Jodie, instead looked down at the magazine in her hands.

Chapter 32

Detectives Samuel Cleaver, Cassie Newell and Drew Hood stood in the small observation room looking through the mirrored window into the interview room. They could see Jodie, but she would not have been able to see them, even if she had bothered to look up.

'Still nothing, not a word out of her?' Cassie asked, with an almost concerned look in her dark blue eyes.

'Not a single syllable, grunt or bark' Samuel replied with a smirk as he ran his hand through his short red hair.

'Oh, come on, that's not fair' Cassie replied.

Drew picked up Jodie's file off the small desk next to him. He opened it and looked down at the paperwork, trying to ignore the impending argument between Cassie and Sam that had been raging on and off ever since Jodie was discovered in that horror-filled basement.

'Really? Have you not read the report of what

she did to all those people?!' Sam replied, with real conviction in his voice.

Cassie was leaning against the side wall just looking at Jodie, she scowled at Sam. She turned back to look at Jodie as she continued to twirl her long dark blonde hair around her fingers, she sighed and then said 'It takes a lot of strength to decapitate someone. Look at the size of her, she must have used her "Primal Strength"…'

'Oh, come on, you sound like one of those shrinks' Sam cut in.

'Just think about it for a moment, if she hadn't taken those teeth, we wouldn't have been able to link all the murders together. Especially the last two.' Cassie interjected.

'Yeah. The old guy Max finally cracked and admitted that he hadn't killed that guy in his living room after he'd been confronted with the other guy buried out back of the Sargent's old place. There hadn't been enough time for him to bury that guy and then get back inside. Besides he'd been too banged up to have buried him' Drew said as he looked up from Jodie's file in his hands.

'Oh, that house would've given me nightmares and she chose to live there with those occupied coffins!' Sam said.

'It's not like she had a lot of options, Sam.'

Cassie replied and then continued with 'the Samson's had a long reach and deep pockets, but even they weren't game to traffic the last of the Fielders. Jodie might've been unwanted by the last of her family but that tree has roots so deep they go back to the very beginning of this town…'

'Yep, that's why she was cut loose instead of being sold, like so many others were.' Drew cut in. He hoped to stop another argument erupting.

'Yeah, until she killed her Great Aunt…' Sam almost shouted at them.

'Who abused her…' Cassie reminded him tersely.

'Yeah, but while the old bat lived, Jodie wasn't worth anything…' Sam countered.

'True.' Cassie conceded.

'When Great Aunty Wendy bought it at the very hands of her own Grandniece, Jodie became very valuable and I bet the Monroe brothers were sent to find and collect her.' Sam said.

'Jodie had been bounced from place to place growing up. It pretty much isolated her and also damaged her, so much so that she wouldn't have realized that her family heritage had given her so much protection…' Drew interjected.

'Although she was a serial killing nutcase by then.' Sam continued, ignoring Drew.

'Don't.' Cassie said.

'Okay, which is probably why the Judge has

already handed down her ruling. Jodie Marie Sargent will spend the rest of her life in our own state-run Psychiatric Facility in the Maximum-Security Ward.' Drew informed them.

'Oh goodie, all those shrinks that have been salivating since she was released from the hospital will be able to annoy the shit out of them and get the fuck out of our hair.' Sam said with sarcastic glee.

'There are some good things to come out of all of this, lots of loose ends can now be tidied up. The missing person cases will dramatically decrease in this state, once they start identifying those remains found out the back of the Smythe's property. So many people who are way too comfortable in their lives are about to have a very rude awakening in the next couple of days when the raids start. Thanks to the records Sebastian Nelson kept we didn't even need to try and flip Martha or Jon Samson on each other. All that information will be bringing down some really big players in child prostitution and trafficking. I still can't believe it worked out so well that neither of them got to make a deal. But I think the best bit was that the Judge has awarded all of Jodie Sargent's inheritance to go to those she nominated. That money will help keep those oldies safe and in their own homes until they die. Then the state will get whatever's left' Drew said. He continued

'Are you ready? Do you really want to do this? I mean it's a long shot, when people go into a Dissociative Shutdown State like this, they very rarely come out again. She must have been laying on that basement floor for about three days before she was found' Drew said as he looked at Cassie.

'It's the last thing that we need to add to her file before she's transported over to the Psychiatric Facility' Cassie said as she pushed herself away from the wall, straightened her shoulders, picked up a plastic cup and a paper bag off the desk. 'Time to do this, Dr Rose Weatherby believes that this might be the only way to get her to respond, we might as well try it' Cassie said with more confidence than she felt.

Drew reached out and gave her shoulder a squeeze as she walked by him. She looked up at him and smiled when she saw the look of concern in his brown eyes.

Cassie walked out of the room and in through the door of the interview room. Inside Jodie sat looking at her hands. She put the cup on the table, Jodie didn't move. Cassie put the paper bag down and then opened it and took out a tooled leather pouch.

Cassie was being so careful with the pouch that she was taken off guard when she looked over and saw Jodie was looking at it. Cassie opened it and carefully poured the contents out into the cup. The teeth fell out making small noises as they fell to the bottom of the cup and then against one another. The sound made Cassie's stomach churn.

Once the pouch was empty, she put it down and asked Jodie one simple word.

'Why?'

Jodie didn't shift her focus from the cup of teeth but said in a flat voice, 'So they couldn't smile their false promises anymore' Jodie smiled at the cup then her face went blank and her eyes dead. She looked back down at her hands.

Cassie knew most of Jodie Marie Sargent's unfortunate life story, she stood there looking at Jodie. She knew she wasn't going to get anything else out of her. She picked up the empty paper bag, leather pouch and the plastic cup full of both real and false teeth. She didn't like the feel of the leather pouch, and it smelt like death. She had been there when they found it around Jodie's neck, sitting close to her skin. It creeped her out thinking about it now.

Cassie turned and walked out of the room and back into the small observation room where the other two Detectives waited.

'Well, that was fruitful' Sam said with a sneer.

'Look, look guys' Drew said as he pointed to Jodie in the room.

There was more life about her slack face. Jodie still looked at her hands in her lap but now she flexed her fingers on her left hand almost like she was holding hands with someone and then she smiled.

****

Jodie was thinking about how she had done so much to save herself and others and here she sat alone. Just waiting to see if they stuck her in a nut house or the big house. All alone, either way, alone. Then she saw Shadow's hand appear under her left hand and clasp it. Shadow said *'We were never alone, we have each other, we always did and always will.'*

****

They all took one more look at the small girl, smiling down on her hand clasping air as they walked out of the room. The Detectives didn't know what to make of what they had just seen.